Had he taken leave of his senses?

How the hell was he going to explain to Carl that he had taken off with one of the prime suspects? His friend would think he was crazy. Maybe he was. But he knew he would do anything, pay anything, to keep Liza out of trouble with the law, and if that made him a fool, then so be it.

Liza was a walking, talking sex goddess. Either dressed in trousers and top with her glorious hair scraped back in a ponytail, as he had seen her this morning, or—with her hair a tumbled mass around her shoulders—elegant in a black wraparound dress that was just begging to be unwrapped. Crook or not, she turned him on without even trying.

To hell with it! He swore. Keeping her out of jail did not mean he had to keep her out of his bed....

To the rescue…armed with a ring!

Modern-Day Knights

Marriage is their mission!

Look for the next thrilling title in this
adventurous new series.

The Yuletide Engagement
by
Carole Mortimer

On sale in December, #2364

Coming soon from
Harlequin Presents

Jacqueline Baird

AT THE SPANIARD'S PLEASURE

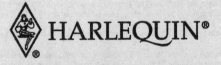

TORONTO • NEW YORK • LONDON
AMSTERDAM • PARIS • SYDNEY • HAMBURG
STOCKHOLM • ATHENS • TOKYO • MILAN • MADRID
PRAGUE • WARSAW • BUDAPEST • AUCKLAND

ISBN 0-373-12337-X

AT THE SPANIARD'S PLEASURE

First North American Publication 2003.

Copyright © 2003 by Jacqueline Baird.

Visit us at www.eHarlequin.com

Printed in U.S.A.

CHAPTER ONE

NICK MENENDEZ irritably drummed his fingers on the steering wheel of the Jeep he had picked up at the airport. He had expected to be in Lanzarote by nine at the latest. He'd arrived in his own plane and he was still late because there'd been no landing slot. Heads would roll... He was a man who got what he wanted when he wanted it, and he did not appreciate being frustrated by anything or anyone! But he should have guessed, he thought, his mouth tightening angrily. Any damn thing connected to Liza Summers, a blonde, blue-eyed siren, had always caused him frustration of one kind or another...

A wry smile twisted his firm lips. No, if he was being honest, his frustration was not really Liza's fault. They had been good friends years ago until he had caught her kissing a young man, and overreacted. With hindsight he could admit it; he had been jealous as hell, he had wanted to be Liza's first lover, but, as he was engaged to someone else at the time, he had been in no position to do anything about it.

Then, last night at his home in Malaga, he had been reading the latest report from one of his companies, a security firm that was doing some work for a pal of his, when her name had leapt off the page.

Last month Carl Dalk, a friend from his university days whose family owned a diamond mine in South Africa, had contacted him and asked for his help and he had immediately agreed. As students they had been white-water rafting together when Nick was thrown from the raft and knocked unconscious. It was Carl who had dragged him from the

5

raging torrent; he owed the man his life. And though they saw each other infrequently, they'd remained good friends.

Nick had joined his father in the family firm straight after university, a small but one of the most prestigious merchant banks in Spain. Over the years Nick had expanded and diversified the business into the vast international corporation it was today. Carl was one of the few people who knew that one of Nick's holdings was a very discreet security agency. It was an agency that had assisted in many sensitive investigations, both corporate and criminal, worldwide, and liaised on a regular basis with the Spanish government on matters of security.

Carl had called on Nick's security firm because twice in the past year diamonds had been stolen from the mine. The clever part was after the thieves had ascertained the value of the diamonds they had been offered back to Carl's insurers at roughly half their worth.

With the consent of the police, and in the hope of catching the thieves red-handed, the insurance company had arranged to pay up. Not surprisingly, as it meant the insurers saved money by not having to repay the full cost of the diamonds. But it had not stopped the insurance company putting up the cost of Carl's premiums, but, worse than that, the plan had not worked...

Both times the thieves after exchanging the diamonds had managed to give the authorities the slip.

Carl's business was in real trouble; what with the influx of cheaper diamonds from Russia over the last few years, and the invention of man-made diamonds, he had seen his firm's profits slump to an all-time low. The drastic fall in the stock market over the same period had seriously depleted the firm and family funding. Carl had a serious cashflow problem and now there had been another theft... Nick had offered to help him out financially, and had put the expertise of the security agency at Carl's disposal.

Reading the last report, Nick had been confident that this time Carl with the help of the agency and the Spanish police were well on the way to catching the thieves, and then he spotted the name Liza Summers. He had called the manager of the security firm, and discovered that it was none other than THE Liza Summers, the daughter of his mother's best friend.

Nick had promised to spend the whole weekend in Spain with his mother to attend a series of parties arranged to celebrate the golden-wedding anniversary of her brother, Uncle Thomas. That plan was seriously curtailed when he'd decided to take the place of his top investigator, and make a flying visit to Lanzarote. If anyone was going to question Liza it was going to be him. It was six years since he had seen her, but whatever else she had become he found it hard to believe she could be involved in these thefts as the report suggested.

Which was why it was now almost eleven and he was stuck at the crossing to the drawbridge in Arrecife as a group of tourists, obviously from the cruise ship in the harbour, made their way over the road. Usually he loved visiting Lanzarote, also known as *Isla de las Volcanoes*. The landscape was surreal, completely covered by over a hundred and thirty volcanoes, with craters and fields of petrified lava. He had owned a villa here for years on the edge of the Timanfaya National Park, as did the king of Spain and the crowned heads of a few Arab countries. It was a place that allowed him to relax out of the public eye and do his own thing. But not today, he thought grimly, his irritation increasing by the minute at the thought of what lay ahead.

The information that had brought Nick dashing to the island caused deep frown lines in his austere but strikingly handsome face as his gaze swept over the scene before him. His hard glance flickered over the kiosk café on the promenade to the taxi rank, where another hold-up was causing chaos. Then abruptly returned to the café, his dark eyes flaring then narrowing on the single female seated at one of the tables.

Long blonde hair tied back with a scarf revealed an exquisite profile, a slender throat and the soft curves of high,
firm breasts exposed by a body-hugging blue cotton top. A
glimpse of bare midriff, then white cotton trousers moulded
long legs that were stretched out before her and crossed at
the ankles in casual ease.

His great body tensed. Well! Well! His information was
correct, he thought with grim satisfaction.

Carl and the South African police had managed to trail
the diamond thieves up through Africa to the Sahara Desert
and discovered they then made the short sea-crossing to the
island of Lanzarote, where they had disappeared either at
sea or on the island. Dalk could have picked up the African
thieves, but that was not what he wanted. He wanted the
top man in Europe to stop it completely.

The report Nick had read last night from his agency had
stated, after they had done some digging on the continent,
the trail led to one Henry Brown, a director of Stubbs and
Company of London, a well-respected investment house.
The top investigator had trailed Henry Brown and discovered he had flown into Lanzarote that day with his PA.

Grinding his teeth in exasperation at the hold-up, Nick
still couldn't get over the fact the man's PA was none other
than Liza Summers. The girl he had known since the age
of eight had become the woman now reclining in the chair
at the promenade café looking as if she did not have a care
in the world... That was about to alter if she did but know
it.

Carl Dalk had received a copy of the same report and
had been on the telephone to Nick late last night, jubilant
as they had almost all the information to spring the trap.
The middleman in Lanzarote was the only missing link.
Still reeling from shock at the sight of Liza's name, Nick
had had to do some very fast talking to persuade Carl to
let him get personally involved and quiz her himself.
Laying it on thick about his connection with the island's
police and telling Carl that he had to go anyway to check

out a business venture, Nick had made arrangements to travel here at once on his private jet.

It was a conflict of interest Nick could do without. He supported Carl a hundred per cent. It was stealing, blackmail, call it what one liked. But he did not want to believe Liza Summers was involved, and if the worst happened and she was, though he could never condone dishonesty, he had to try and keep her part in the theft low-key and out of the Press. He owed it to the family friendship and the delightful child she had once been.

Eyes black as night raked over her once again, his firm lips curling in a wolfish grin, there was nothing childish about her now. Nick was something of a connoisseur of beautiful women and this one certainly fitted the bill. Things were certainly looking up, he decided; the idea of quizzing the lovely Liza was suddenly very tempting.

Nick watched as the woman removed her sunglasses and looked towards him. No, not him but the drawbridge, he realised, and his hands tightened on the steering wheel at the same time as he felt a sudden tightening in his groin. There was no doubt about it. It was Liza Summers…

His body's instant reaction surprised him. He had not responded so spontaneously to a female in a long time. He was famed for his cool control and he rather resented his body's betrayal, but finding Liza so quickly was the first bit of luck he had had all morning. An accidental meeting was much more convenient than calling at her hotel. He had not seen the woman in six years, and if anything she was even more beautiful then he remembered, on the outside at least, he qualified cynically, remembering the task at hand.

Damn the law! He parked the Jeep at the side of the road and leapt out.

'Liza… Liza Summers…'

Liza clashed her coffee-cup down on the saucer, the deep, drawling voice making her hand shake. Oh, no! Silently

she groaned. This could not be happening. She hadn't heard
that voice since she was a teenager. Now, on a tiny island
in the middle of the Atlantic it echoed in her head like a
ghost from the past.

'I thought it was you.'

A tall, dark shadow loomed over her, blocking out the
sun. Her eyes were on a level with strong masculine thighs
clad in denim. She swallowed hard and slowly lifted her
head; a tapered waist flared out to a broad chest, every
muscle and sinew clearly delineated by a simple black
T-shirt, and up to bulging biceps, and even broader shoulders.

She tilted her head back, and her heart skipped a beat;
his face was in shadow but she would have recognised him
anywhere. 'You!' she exclaimed as her blue eyes clashed
with deep dark brown. Niculoso Menendez... The years
rolled back and she was eight again and meeting him for
the first time.

Her father had just died and her mum's good friend Anna
Menendez had invited Liza and her mother, Pamela, for a
holiday at her home in Spain. The two women had attended
the same boarding-school in England. Anna was the daughter of a Spanish diplomat and Pamela was the daughter of
a serving army officer. Anna had married a wealthy
Spaniard and Pam had married an army man. The two
women had kept in touch over the years, mostly as pen
pals.

Memories of the past flooded Liz's mind. Niculoso had
fascinated her the first time she saw him, at eighteen he
was the most beautiful young man she had ever seen. She
had been so busy staring at him that she had stumbled and
fallen on the stone-flagged courtyard, skinning her knee.
She had cried, but Niculoso had picked her up, smiled at
her and carried her on his shoulders into the imposing
house.

He had been her hero from that moment on. He was the
big brother she had never had and she had looked forward

to the three weeks at the Menendez country house every summer.

'Do you mind if I join you? I haven't seen you in years.' Nick's deep, husky voice cut across her reverie.

'What?' she mumbled, still reeling from the shock of his sudden appearance. It was Nick who had taught her to ride, and saved her from many a fall from trees, cliffs, and on one memorable occasion when she had fallen from her horse. But at fourteen her feelings for him had changed when she had developed an enormous crush on him, and done everything in her power to try and attract his attention to her blossoming femininity.

'You don't sound too pleased to see me.' Nick lifted a hand and signalled to the waiter and ordered a coffee. 'Would you like a refill?'

'No… Yes…' she stammered like an idiot, but she was stunned. He had appeared from nowhere like a genie out of a bottle, filling her mind with kaleidoscopic memories.

Their past relationship had ended in disaster when she was sixteen. Overflowing with unrequited love, she had been devastated when she was introduced to Nick's fiancée, a stunningly attractive woman called Sophia, a distant relative of the family.

Suddenly Liza had seen her mother and herself for what they were. The poor friends who were given a holiday out of charity. That summer she had rebelled and gone out with one of the stable boys. It was just her bad luck the one time they were fooling around in an empty stall and she had let him kiss her, Nick had seen them. Nick with a face like thunder…

An involuntary shiver feathered down her spine, and her heartbeat quickened perceptibly. She did not want to think about what had happened next. But the scales had certainly fallen from her eyes where Nick was concerned. Nick Menendez was an arrogant, overbearing, stuck-up, chauvinist pig. Liza had kept out of his way for the rest of her stay, and if he had happened to see her he frowned at her with contempt obvious in his hard eyes. Liza had been relieved when they finally left and she'd never gone back.

Shaking her head in an attempt to dispel the memories of the past, she glanced up at him. He had moved slightly and the sun glinted off his striking features, and her heart stopped in her throat.

One dark brow arched enquiringly. 'So may I sit down?' His voice was a deep, slightly accented drawl that held a hint of mockery.

'Please do,' she finally managed to respond civilly. Though she was still shocked at the amazing coincidence of bumping into Niculoso in Lanzarote. Since the death of his father she guessed he had inherited the family company. She had seen his name in the gossip columns occasionally, when he'd attended a charity do, a première or the races, and grimaced at the reference to the Spanish Stud, supposedly a reference to the famous Menendez stud farm, but the *double entendre* was obvious. Still, Liza tried to avoid reading such rubbish.

'The last time we met must have been my father's funeral,' Nick prompted, pulling out a chair.

'Oh, yes,' Liza murmured politely. That was another day she would rather forget. She had just turned nineteen and was at university in London, and living in the halls of residence. Her mum had insisted Liza travel to Spain with her for the funeral. Nick had still been engaged to the glorious Sophia and Liza had found him just as disturbing then, and when he had deigned to notice her his expression was still one of scowling contempt.

Liza hadn't seen him since. She wished he would sit down instead of holding the chair and towering over her like some great, dark bird of prey. He was smiling down at her like a long-lost friend, and somehow it didn't ring true. A vulture about to pick her bones was more likely, she thought drily.

'Well, Niculoso, fancy meeting you here,' she said

coolly, her mind spinning. 'I thought you lived in Antequera.'

'My mother still does. But I am a big boy now, Liza. I left home years ago,' he drawled mockingly, and finally sat down beside her. He *was* big and he *was* more striking than ever, she realised, her skin breaking out in goose-pimples as his arm accidentally brushed hers.

'As, I believe, did you after university,' Nick continued, apparently casually. A large hand reached out and covered her much smaller one resting on the table, and to her amazement something akin to an electric shock sizzled up her arm. 'My mother speaks about you often and it is really good to see you again,' he said and squeezed her hand.

Good to see her! He had to be kidding... He could not stand the sight of her... Liza felt the colour rise in her cheeks. She had told herself she hated him for years and yet incredibly his touch sent a *frisson* of excitement flooding through her. Her stunned blue gaze clashed with deep dark brown—was it sincerity she saw in their depths? Never in a million years... She wasn't falling for his Latin charm ever again. 'Yes. Well...' she murmured inconsequentially.

'Forgive me for surprising you. I caught a glimpse of you and could not believe my eyes. You have developed into a stunning woman, Liza.'

Niculoso Menendez giving her a compliment! He had to be joking after the scathing things he had said about her in the past. 'Thank you, I think,' she said with a trace of sarcasm. She pulled her hand free from beneath his and lowered her eyes from his too astute gaze.

Liza remembered all too well every second of their encounter in the stable years ago.

After dispensing with the stable boy, Nick had hauled her hard against him and kissed her savagely, and to her undying shame she had responded in a way she had never imagined in her wildest dreams, clinging to him like a limpet. Then he had shoved her back into the stall, and insolently touched her tight breasts, and completely humiliated her. His words were engraved on her brain.

'*My God! A stable boy! How wrong I was about you. For two years I have watched you flirt and flaunt yourself around me. I thought it was innocent, a young girl learning the power of her emerging sexuality. But you obviously know it all, have done it all. You're nothing but a cheap slut.*'

The memory still had the power to hurt, but Liza drew some consolation from the fact that, young as she was, at least she'd had the sense to slap his arrogant face.

Nick leant back in his seat and eyed the woman before him. She had been a delightful, impulsive child, a thorn in his flesh as a very independent, precocious teenager, and a bitter disappointment to him when he'd found her cavorting with the stable boy. But she had developed into an exquisitely beautiful woman, and he didn't like the way she still affected him after years of blanking her from his mind. His gut reaction last night when he'd realised she was involved had been to protect her any way he could, and the strength of his own feeling had surprised him.

But he was no fool; she had inherited her mother's features and pale, almost translucent skin, and at the moment the red tinge to her cheeks and the evasive look in her brilliant blue eyes told him she was as guilty as hell about something. Whether it was because she was involved in the theft of the diamonds or not he did not know, but he was determined to find out for Carl's sake.

'I can see life has been good to you, Liza,' Nick opined, his dark eyes sweeping over her face and lower to the soft curve of her breasts with blatant male appreciation. 'It is great to see you happy and on holiday.'

'Yes, well, the sunshine is a treat in the winter,' Liza offered lightly. She was older and wiser now, and not prepared to accept his friendly overtures so easily.

Nick's gaze narrowed intently on her lovely face, and he saw the swift tightening of her luscious lips; she was being evasive—hardly the reaction of an innocent, he was forced to conclude. 'You *are* on holiday?' he queried, pressing on in an attempt to discover exactly what Liza knew. 'Or is it business? It has been so long since we last saw each other, I have no idea what you are up to now.' For a fleeting moment he was tempted to ask, *A bit of diamond-smuggling, perhaps, as my agency's report implies?* His lips twitched in the briefest smile at the thought.

The shock of meeting Niculoso Menendez was wearing off a little and, seeing his smile, Liza thought there was no harm in discussing her work. 'I'm a PA for a director of a finance firm in London.' It was a safe topic, and she told him the name of the firm. 'As for this,' she gestured with one hand around the bay, 'it started out as a business trip to attend an environmental conference at Costa Teguise in the hope of investing in something green, I suppose, but surprisingly it has ended up as a holiday for me. My boss has a habit of changing his mind,' Liza ended drily, something she was quickly discovering in the few weeks she had worked for Mr Brown.

She had arrived on the island yesterday with her boss. They were staying at a five-star hotel on the Costa Teguise to attend the two-week conference. But, after vanishing last night before dinner, Henry Brown had appeared this morning and informed her that, after reading the literature, the conference was of no importance to the firm.

Instead he had asked her to do him a favour and deliver a package to an opticians in Arrecife, the island's capital, then take the rest of the time off. He told her she could stay in the hotel, as it was paid for, or go wherever she liked. Just to make sure she was around for the gala dinner on the final evening, and to take the flight back with him the day after.

He was going sailing, but would be back the morning of the gala. Plus, if his wife happened to call and catch Liza, Liza was to tell her he had been called away suddenly.

Liza had argued she was not prepared to lie to his wife,

until he pointed out she was his PA now after four years of being the secretary to Mr Stubbs, who had recently retired. It was the first time she had travelled with him, and if she valued her job she had better get used to obeying his orders. Liza had a sneaky suspicion he had arranged the whole trip so he could slope off with his latest mistress.

Something green! Nick almost snorted. The only thing green Henry Brown was interested in was a green-back dollar... Liza could not be that naive...

'Lucky for you,' he prompted, his attitude towards her hardening. So she was not a complete liar, but she was extremely clever—enough of the truth mixed with fiction, Nick thought cynically, his dark eyes roaming once more over her face and body. He wondered if Liza was sleeping with her boss. She had been heading that way at sixteen, and he could not see any red-blooded male turning her down. Immediately he pushed the vaguely distasteful thought aside.

'Yes,' Liza agreed coolly. Henry Brown was supposedly a happily married man, but he had hit on her the first week she started work for the company, but, firmly rebuffed, he had accepted with good grace and over the years they had developed a formal working relationship.

Henry Brown was a charming rogue who was probably an asset in the world of venture capitalism, but not really husband material. Still, his private life was not her problem...she was not her boss's moral guardian, she told herself firmly.

The waiter arrived with the coffee and Liza picked up the cup and took a sip of the aromatic brew. She could feel Nick's dark gaze on her as the silence lengthened between them. But she saw no reason why she should carry the conversation. She had not instigated this meeting with him.

Twenty minutes ago, after delivering the package, she had sat down at this table, drunk a cup of coffee, and told herself she was going to enjoy the unexpected break. It was magic to be able to sit outside in the middle of January with the temperature a balmy seventy-eight degrees after the winter gloom she had left in England. Now she was not so sure…. Suddenly it felt a whole lot warmer, and she set the coffee-cup down with a less than steady hand. She could not believe Nick was actually sitting beside her, and, worse, affecting her usual icy composure like no other man before.

'I have heard of Stubbs; a very profitable firm, I believe,' Nick finally remarked.

Startled, Liza took a moment to remember what they had been talking about.

'Your mother must be very proud of your success; though I hate to admit it, I have only seen her a couple of times in the last few years, usually when she is visiting my mother. It is a shame you never come with her any more,' Nick offered lightly. He had caught the flash of panic in her eyes, and wondered why. His comment had been harmless enough. Liza was an elegant, sophisticated woman now, but that flash of fear simply confirmed his mounting suspicion she was hiding something.

'Some time, maybe,' Liza replied shortly. She needed no reminding of her holidays at his home, and asked, 'And what are you doing here? I thought you still lived in Spain.'

'I just flew in this morning. I have a villa here, though I have a house in Malaga, and of course the family home, but my business takes me all over the world.'

'How nice,' Liza murmured. 'What is it you actually do?' she queried sarcastically. Apart from flitting around the world in a private jet, usually with a glamorous woman on your arm, she almost added, but resisted the temptation.

If ever a child was born with a silver spoon in his mouth it was Niculoso Menendez. The only son of one of the wealthiest families on the continent, he lived a charmed life, indulging his every whim, whether it was skydiving, bunjee jumping or snowboarding in the Alps. He was an exponent of extreme sports, and she had thought his adventures so brave and romantic as a child. But raking over the past was churning up memories she preferred to forget, and, pinning a smile on her face she forced herself to look up into his eyes.

For a second she thought she saw a flash of anger in their depths, but she was quickly reassured when his firmly chiselled lips parted over gleaming white teeth in a reciprocal smile that was meant to dazzle…and did…

'Right at this moment I am talking to a beautiful woman,' he said smoothly, 'when I should be checking a property development on the other side of the island.'

'So you're a property developer. That must be interesting,' she prompted, jumping at the chance to change the subject. Niculoso complimenting her, flirting with her, made her uncomfortable. 'I seem to remember you studied art, wasn't it? But your father was in finance, I believe,' she opined with the lift of one delicately shaped eyebrow. And Nick had stood to inherit the lot, and marry the family-approved distant relative, Sophia, Liza recalled cynically.

'You're right and he was, but with my father's backing we diversified into other areas, though property development is one of my own pet projects.'

Surprisingly Liza believed him. There was no mistaking the passion in his tone, the gleam of determination in his incredible eyes as he expanded on the subject.

'For instance, here on Lanzarote the landscape fascinates me. It is quite challenging to build something that is pleasing to the eye, and yet does not harm the unique environment. Don't get me wrong. I am not one of those dyed-in-the-wool environmentalists. I do enjoy the better things of life.'

Liza just bet he did! Her blue eyes lingered on his harshly handsome face, the deliciously mobile mouth, a wry smile tugging her lips. He wasn't called the Spanish Stud for nothing…

'But here no building must be more than four storeys, mainly from the lobbying of the late, great Cesar Manrique, a famous local sculptor. You have probably seen some of his work around the island.'

'I've read about him, but I only arrived yesterday afternoon and I haven't had a chance to look around yet,' Liza said, her smile broadening as for a moment she caught a glimpse of the eighteen-year-old he had once been. A young man full of high ideals and not above expounding them to a young child, before maturity and money had made him the man he was today.

'In that case, Liza, you must allow me to be your guide for the day,' Nick declared, flashing her another dazzling smile. Her heart lurched and for a moment she simply stared at him. 'That is, if you are alone, of course,' he prompted softly.

His deep, velvet voice trickled over her nerve-endings like dark gold honey, soothing and seducing. 'Yes. Yes, I am,' she stammered.

He really was a hunk of a man and the years since they had last met had been kind to him. If anything he was more attractive than she remembered, age giving character to his stunningly handsome face, with perfectly carved features, high cheekbones and a sensually curved mouth. As for his eyes, deep brown and as dark as sin with thick black curling lashes. The kind of eyes that would melt any female's heart and the slightly long, silky black hair would tempt any female's fingers. Liza was no exception; she wasn't even aware she was staring and she never saw the brief glitter of triumph in his gorgeous eyes.

Nick Menendez's physical presence was almost hypnotic; he exuded a lethal charm, an aura of potent masculine sexuality that called out to every atom of femininity in a woman. On a scale of one to ten, he had to be a twenty. Liza almost groaned out loud as all her deeply buried teenage fantasies rose up to haunt her.

'I'm amazed.' His eyes twinkled. 'A lovely girl like you, alone! But grateful.' Her blue eyes widened to their fullest extent on his darkly attractive face at his teasing compliment. 'So, unless you would like another coffee, how about joining me in the Jeep?' A strong hand gestured to where the vehicle was illegally parked on the pavement. 'Before some official tows it away. I have to inspect the building site but after that I am at your disposal.'

If only! A vivid image of a naked Nick at her disposal filled her head and, ashamed of her sexy thoughts, she answered hastily. 'I was going to return to my hotel and laze around the pool.' She was still slightly wary of this new, charming Nick. Over the years she'd worked hard to block out any sign of emotion where this man was concerned, and she wasn't sure she liked the way he cut through her defences like a knife through butter with just a smile.

He had been scathing in his contempt of her, brutally so, in the past. So why the turn-around, the flattering comments now? she wondered. Nick was a powerful, dynamic man; add wealth and looks, and it wasn't surprising he was so arrogantly sure of himself. But surely he must be married by now with a handful of children, yet her mother had never mentioned it. 'And maybe your wife, Sophia, would object.' Fool, fool, she castigated herself as soon as the words had left her mouth.

Hooded eyes narrowed intently on her slightly pink face. Nick was a man of considerable expertise where the female sex was concerned, and despite her cautious reserve he sensed an underlying attraction. She wanted him, and the question on his marital state confirmed it. 'Sophia and I parted years ago. I have no wife, no ties, and I like it that way. Now, no more argument.' Nick rose to his feet and held out his hand. 'Come on, you know you want to,' he opined with sheer masculine arrogance and a wicked grin. 'I have been reliably informed I am a charming companion. Surely you would not want to disappoint me and dent my fragile ego.'

Liza grinned back; she couldn't help it. 'That would be an impossibility,' she mocked. 'But surely a man in your position must have better things to do than spend a day sightseeing with me,' and she nearly added *of all people*. Memories of the past made her super-cautious; Nick had made his dislike of her very plain, and she was still not convinced of his sincerity now.

'Are you still angry with me?' Shrewd dark eyes bored down into hers, guessing the reason for her hesitation. 'For lecturing you as a child?'

Lecturing her! So that was how little he thought of crushing her burgeoning sexuality under a diatribe of insults and a savage kiss and grope. But with the benefit of maturity Liza wondered if maybe he was right, and she had made too much of what had happened. 'No, of course not,' she denied. If he could be so casual about their fight, then so could she, and, putting her hand in his, she allowed him to pull her to her feet. Liza was tall at five feet nine, but Nick towered over her, and she had to tilt her head back to look at him. 'Why should I be?' she asked, and suddenly she was conscious of the nearness of his great, virile physique, but was incapable of moving away.

'No reason at all,' Nick drawled throatily, pinning her with a smouldering glance, and after a provocative pause added, 'not now.' He lifted her hand to rest on his broad chest, and she felt the heat of his flesh through his shirt, and involuntarily she shivered. 'What is not acceptable in a girl of sixteen does not apply to the beautiful woman you have become,' he declared huskily and gazed at her, his eyes smouldering with an explicit sensual promise.

Liza stiffened slightly. Nick was as arrogant as ever; he would not come on to a teenager, but an older woman was fair game. Why was she surprised? In a way he was quite moral, she thought wryly. Then his long fingers tightened on her hand, the pad of his thumb caressing her palm, and she stopped thinking altogether.

'So unless there is somewhere else you need to go,' he urged her along the pavement, 'any shopping or more errands to run for your boss...?' He stopped and trailed off.

'No, no,' Liza denied, not quite sure what she was denying—his question or her helpless response to him. 'Work finished when I dropped a package off for my boss at Daidolas in the town this morning, just before I met you actually.'

'Daidolas the opticians?' Nick asked swiftly.

'Yes, that's right, I think it was probably some glasses,' she babbled on, intensely aware of him with every beat of her heart. 'My time is my own from now on.' She saw his dark eyes flicker with some emotion she did not recognise, and felt the sudden tension in his tall frame, and her hand trembled in his. 'So thank you for your kind invitation, Niculoso,' she heard herself say with ridiculous formality in an attempt to hide the chaotic feelings his nearness aroused in her, and snatched her hand free from his, dying with embarrassment.

Then she gasped as two large hands closed around her waist, and she was lifted off her feet and spun around, a hard, warm mouth briefly brushed her lips, and then she was in the Jeep.

'So polite, Liza,' he drawled mockingly. 'Please, we are old friends and my friends call me Nick.' And, chuckling at her flushed, bemused expression, he added, 'Fasten your seat belt,' before strolling around the front of the car and stepping into the driving seat.

'My friends call me Liza,' she muttered distractedly, still reeling from the touch of his mouth on her own, as he started the engine.

Nick cast her a glance, a broad grin lighting his tanned face. 'I did know that, Liza,' he mocked her. The speed with which she had offered the information he required meant his mission would not be as difficult as he had thought. 'I just have to make a call.' He gestured with his mobile. 'The reception is better away from the traffic.' And he jumped back out of the Jeep and strolled a few yards to the beach. He was taking no chances on Liza overhearing. Damn! But she was good. By revealing her actions so readily, either she really was simply an innocent messenger, or a consummate actress.

It may have been glass in the package! But not of the optical variety...he would bet his last cent.

Quickly he called Carl and gave him the information about the drop-off point and then talked Carl out of having Liza picked up immediately by persuading him it made more sense for Nick to keep her with him on the off-chance she had more information of use to them.

What troubled him slightly as he leapt back into the Jeep was why he was so keen to believe in her innocence. A man of his wealth, and bachelor status, he was used to the adulation of women and was wise to all their tricks to entrap him; consequently he had a very cynical attitude to the female sex in general, but Liza confused him... Not an emotion he was comfortable with.

Liza wriggled deeper into the seat as Nick flashed her a brief smile before driving away. She glanced down at his elegant, bronzed hand wrapped around the gear stick, saw the sinews in his strong arms flex as he changed gear, and thought of the same hand on her breast.

Oh, hell! She silently groaned. What a time to start having erotic thoughts about the man. She must remember Nick thought he was miles above her in every way; he had made that very plain years ago. She had to try and relax and enjoy the day for what it was. Two old friends sharing a tour of the island. It was sheer coincidence they had even met again. But in that she was wrong...

CHAPTER TWO

'FIRE MOUNTAIN; I can see why,' Liza said softly, staring around in awe. After a brief visit to a building site, Nick had driven Liza into the national park, passing a trail of about fifty camels, provided to give rides to the tourists. But Nick had taken them up into what looked like a lunar landscape. At first she had thought it was the sun shining off the lava that made it appear red, but the further they went she realised it was the rock itself that was red.

Nick stopped the Jeep and lifted her down, keeping one hand around her waist, and she stood in the crook of his arm, not sure which affected her the most—the man or the mountains. She had never seen or felt anything like it in her life. Craters, some huge, some small, the rock red and black and even a trace of green, but not a blade of grass grew there, and the silence was almost spiritual.

'Impressive, hmm?' Nick prompted. 'Some people thought the gods were laughing when the eruptions started on April the first in 1730. It is known as the greatest volcanic holocaust ever witnessed. Thirty-two volcanoes rose up and erupted, spewing forth great quantities of molten rock.' His hand tightened around her waist, his fingers against the bare skin of her midriff guiding her towards a view of five mountains in a line. 'Those five erupted one after the other like Chinese firecrackers apparently. What finally wiped out most of the vegetation was the last eruption in the 1850s.'

Liza felt a bit like erupting herself; she had never been so conscious of a man in her life. She had had boyfriends and one she actually thought she loved, until they'd got engaged and made love for the first time and it was a disaster as far as Liza was concerned, and the end of the relationship. No man had ever affected her the way Nick's simplest touch seemed to do. She had to make a deliberate effort to fight down the stirrings of desire just the sound of his voice aroused in her. Ruthlessly she clamped down on her wayward thoughts, and turned in his hold to look up at him. 'I have never seen anything like it; it is absolutely fascinating.' She smiled.

His heavy-lidded eyes darkened softly on her upturned face. 'So are you, Liza.'

Suddenly the atmosphere was thick with tension. Liza was aware of his hand on her bare midriff, his fingers flexing on her skin, and she knew he was going to kiss her, and then to her surprise he stepped back, setting her free.

'But you ain't seen nothing yet,' Nick joked in a mock-American accent.

Hell! He had almost kissed her. How could he even think of making love with Liza Summers until he knew exactly what she was? The answer came with a tightening in his groin, and, shoving a hand in his trouser pocket, he spun around. 'Come on back to the Jeep.'

She did not know whether she was disappointed or relieved, but from then on the atmosphere between them slipped back into the easygoing camaraderie of years ago.

Nick was an excellent guide and drove them to another tourist vantage point set high in the weird hills. First he dropped some gravel in her hands that was red hot, and she squealed in surprise, and then they watched as an attendant dropped a bush down a ten-foot hole and it immediately caught fire. Then they walked up to the Vulcano restaurant, the only building for miles around.

'I don't believe it.' She shook her head, her blue eyes laughing up at Nick. They were standing by a large circular well in the restaurant, the heat from the earth below rising to barbecue the chicken pieces spread on the iron grill on top.

'Believe it.' Nick took her arm and led her into the dining room. 'You can't visit Lanzarote and not eat volcano-grilled chicken.'

He was right and lunch was a jovial affair shared with dozens of tourists. Liza was amazed how well Nick mixed in; she would not have thought it his scene at all. The jet set were his usual companions according to gossip. But she did not have time to dwell on the point as Nick drove her all around the island. They stopped at a small lagoon, and then it was on again to a great volcanic tunnel and deep caves with pools where tiny blind white crabs lived, the only place on earth other than miles deep in the sea.

Back in the Jeep, the daylight quickly failing, Liza turned laughing eyes up to Nick. 'I can see why you have a villa here; you really love this place.' The hours had flown—Liza had had a great day, and the company had been superb, and all the better for being so unexpected.

'Yes, I come here a lot; it is ideal, as one of my hobbies is seismology,' Nick admitted honestly; he wanted her to feel secure with him and by giving a little more of himself he might get her to trust him, and reveal the depths of her own involvement with the thieves, if any... She was the daughter of his mother's best friend, for heaven's sake, and the longer he spent with Liza the more difficult he found it to believe she was guilty of anything underhand. It was up to him to discover the truth of her involvement, but he was beginning to think she was the unwitting messenger for her sleazy boss.

'That figures, I suppose.' Liza grinned; his effect on her was certainly seismic, she thought privately. And in a way it made sense; at thirty-five perhaps he had swapped extreme sports to study the extremes of nature. 'But do we have to see everything in one day?' she asked, hoping Nick would take the hint and ask her out again.

Nick glanced at her smiling face, his hooded eyes masking his expression. Her lips were begging to be kissed and it took every bit of will-power he possessed to resist the temptation; it was too soon... He needed to make sure her information had been correct. But whether it was or not, his mind was made up—he was going to give Liza the benefit of the doubt. He did not think for a moment she was aware of it, but by coming to Lanzarote she had inadvertently got mixed up with some very nasty criminals, and he was going to do everything in his power to protect her, whether she wanted him to or not. He owed it to their years of friendship, and their mothers'.

'No, of course not. I'll take you back to your hotel now as I have some business to attend to.' He read the flicker of disappointment in her brilliant blue eyes, and almost gave in. His gaze dipped to her mouth, the full, sensuous lips, and he ached to taste them with his own, had done all day... *Dios!* He needed to get a grip—business before pleasure... Later, he promised himself...

Everything was going according to plan. He had kept Liza out of the way all day, and the information she had given him, which he had passed on to Carl over the phone this morning, should have been acted on by now. He needed to contact Carl Dalk again to discover what had happened. 'I'll call back for you at eight and take you to dinner.' And his lips curled in amused satisfaction at the open relief in her smile.

'Nick. Hi. Your information was correct.' Nick Menendez lounged back in the chair at his desk in the study, and listened as Carl's slightly harassed-sounding tones filled the room.

'We visited the opticians and questioned the receptionist, and picked up Daidolas at his home and found the diamonds on him. He sang like a bird. He was a jeweller before he was an optician; he does the valuation and passes the information on to an intermediary in Morocco who makes the arrangements to contact the insurance company, and do the deal.'

'So we have them,' Nick prompted.

'Not quite. As you know, Henry Brown is the top man.

He arranges everything, his company charters a yacht in Marbella on the Spanish mainland, a different one each time, ostensibly for corporate entertainment. But in reality he has the captain pick up the diamonds at appointed places on the African coast and then transport them to Lanzarote.'

Nick grimaced; he had been hoping like hell Liza was not involved, but it wasn't looking good for her. Knowingly or not she had delivered the diamonds. 'So we pick up Henry Brown,' he said quickly.

'Eventually, yes; apparently Brown's one weakness is he cannot resist checking the diamonds himself before they are passed to the optician for valuation. Plus he obviously does not trust the middleman he uses to do the exchange, because on every previous occasion he has been in the same vicinity ready to receive the cash when the deal is done.'

'So what's the problem, Carl?' Nick asked. 'You have him under surveillance; when the time is right, take him.'

'If only it was that easy,' Carl said drily. 'Unfortunately we have lost track of him.'

'You've what?' Nick jerked upright in the chair. 'How the hell did you manage that? I thought you had the police trailing him.'

'Don't yell at me, partner, and we did. They watched him collect the package last night from a yacht in the marina at Teguise, and they knew he had handed it on to the woman this morning.' Nick's frown deepened; he did not like hearing Liza referred to as *the woman*, but he listened as Carl continued. 'They watched as Brown left in the same yacht this morning, but somehow he outsmarted them, vanished off the radar screen. But I doubt very much the thieving bastard sank.'

'We've lost him,' Nick groaned.

'Not to worry, the local police and I have a plan. In the past two incidences, about a week or ten days after the initial contact with the insurance company the cash and diamonds were exchanged once in Morocco and once at sea, as you know. But this time, by some not so friendly questioning of Daidolas we know the exchange is going to be made in Lanzarote. He also gave us the names of a couple of local sailors who have crewed for Brown in the past. The police are tracking them down as we speak. It is only a matter of time and with Daidolas's help, and the promise of leniency, we have set a trap. We are going to keep him locked up over the weekend to give him a taste of what to expect if he does not do as we say, and set him free on Monday under very close supervision. When the deal is done Brown will turn up to cash in, and hopefully we will get the whole gang.'

'It still does not alter the fact you lost him,' Nick almost groaned.

'Hey, it's not that bad, Nick; as long as you still have the girl, the police can question her—she is bound to know something.'

Nick's whole body tensed. His immediate reaction was one of outrage at the thought of Liza being taken to a police station and body-searched before being questioned and probably ending up in a cell. The outrage was followed by a completely alien emotion for him—fear, and then a surge of cold, hard anger. Not if he could help it, he vowed. He closed his eyes briefly and counted to ten, fighting to stay calm before responding casually, 'You can safely leave the girl to me, Carl. If she knows anything at all I will tell you—I am meeting her for dinner later.'

'You're what?' Carl's voice rose a notch. 'Are you crazy? You've left her on her own; she could be miles away by now…she could warn Brown, and the whole deal will go pear-shaped.'

'Come on, Carl, I can assure you Liza will be ready and waiting when I go to pick her up. Have you ever known my Menendez charm to fail?' Nick drawled mockingly. 'A woman has never run away from me in my life, and I can assure you that, after spending the day with Liza, she is no exception.' And he prayed his friend would buy it. He did not question why. He just knew he did not want Liza falling into the police's or Carl's clutches, friend or not.

A husky chuckle greeted Nick's comment. 'You're right, but this is vital, Nick. Make damn sure you get the woman. We need to know where Brown has gone and when he will be back.'

'Don't worry.' Nick ran his free hand distractedly through his dark hair, and was glad they were not on videophone. 'I'll do what it takes to get the information and call you back later with the information you want.'

'You're being very noble. "Do what it takes",' he mocked. 'Good-looking, is she?'

'Certainly no hardship,' Nick joked back. 'Speak to you later.' And he cut the connection, his face as black as thunder.

Striding into the living room, he poured a large measure of whisky into a crystal glass, raised it to his mouth and took a long, fiery drink.

But still a cold knot formed in Nick's belly. Liza Summers; he was not sure if she was guilty or not. The child he had known had been embarrassingly honest. But the beautiful, sophisticated woman of twenty-five she had become... That was a different question. It was perfectly possible she lived by her wits and stunning looks, and her job was just a cover for stealing. On the other hand she could be completely innocent, and, as she had implied, simply following her boss's orders...

He knew he had to question her tonight about Henry Brown, and he also knew he should instruct his people to look into the state of her finances, but somehow he could not bring himself to do it. Maybe because he still held cherished memories of the child she had been.

Nick snorted in disgust and spun round. Who the hell was he kidding? He had taken one look at Liza today, and his body had reacted like a teenager. He had kept her out of the way all day for her own sake, and his if he was honest. Carl would have quite happily had her arrested this morning. Liza was beautiful, granted, but then all Nick's women were beautiful, and he had never felt the slightest need to protect them. So why Liza Summers?

He could tell himself it was for her mother's sake, to avoid the embarrassment a court case would cause, but that was only part of his reasoning. There was no point in pretending; along with surely every man on the planet, he wanted Liza for himself. He had walked around all day in a semi-permanent state of arousal, and he ached with frustration. Right at this moment he would not care if Liza was the biggest thief in Christendom, if he could get her in his bed.

There, he had admitted it. Nick scowled as he lifted the glass in his hand to his mouth again and drained the whisky from it then slammed it down on a convenient table.

Now, get over it…he told himself and walked out of the house, his aristocratic features as hard as granite and his heavy-lidded eyes equally as stony as he slid into the waiting car.

Three hours later, rested and showered, Liza walked back into her bedroom and surveyed the clothes she had brought with her. Excitement and anticipation bubbled in her veins like the finest champagne. She tried to keep a lid on her emotions, but it was difficult, for the first time in years, she was really looking forward to going out with a man. She fantasised in her mind how the night would progress—a candlelit meal somewhere romantic, with a deep conversation verging on the intimate, a few gentle caresses and at evening's end perhaps a kiss, or even more…

She shivered delectably, and took a fourth outfit from the wardrobe. Nick was attracted to her, she knew it, and for once she allowed herself to think of a relationship with a man—not just any man, but Nick Menendez.

He had explained why he had yelled at her at sixteen, it was simply because of her age, and she could understand that even though she did not agree with his chauvinistic attitude. But now he saw her as a mature, sophisticated woman, and he was interested. She had seen it in his eyes, in his touch, and this time she was going to take the chance, and to pot with the consequences. Who knew, she thought optimistically, this could be the start of something big…?

Liza finally settled on a sleeveless, figure-hugging black jersey-silk dress. She slipped it over her shoulders; the bodice crossed over between her breasts and tied around her narrow waist, the wrap-around skirt ending a couple of inches above her knees. But, mindful the nights could be chilly, she added a pashmina shawl in silver-grey.

She left her long hair loose and straight, and with the addition of one more coat of lip-gloss she was ready. She stood back from the mirror. Not bad, she thought, and slipped her feet into high-heeled sandals. She was reaching for her clutch bag when the telephone rang.

It was Reception to say a Niculoso Menendez had arrived. Her heart did a funny little jig in her chest, and, taking a deep breath, she closed the door behind her and crossed to the elevator, her blue eyes sparkling with excited anticipation at the evening ahead.

Liza walked out of the elevator, and saw him immediately. He was leaning against the reception desk, laughing at something the attractive receptionist had said to him. To her surprise she felt a swift stab of something very like jealousy, and just as quickly a stomach-curling pleasure as he turned and saw her.

His firm lips parted over gleaming white teeth in a slow, sensual smile. Liza had thought he looked great in jeans, but, dressed with unexpected severity in a superbly tailored dark suit with a white shirt and plain dark tie, the man possessed a lethal, predatory aura, a supreme confidence in his masculinity that made every fine hair on her skin stand erect.

She couldn't help it; she watched with total fascination as his big, powerfully muscled body moved towards her with a lithe arrogance that made her pulse race with excitement.

He stopped an arm's length away, and Liza swallowed hard. So the man was incredibly handsome, sinfully sexy, and her insides felt as if they were dissolving but it was only a chemical reaction, just lust, she told herself, plain and simple. She was no longer the adoring child who hung on to his every word, but a successful career woman. Involuntarily Liza straightened her shoulders, and stood a little taller. She could handle a date with Nick, and without having a fit of the vapours, she scolded herself, and tilted her chin assertively.

'Nick, so sorry to keep you waiting.'

'You are worth any wait, Liza,' Nick opined throatily. His dark eyes travelled over her from her hair, her face, lower to linger on her cleavage, revealed by the neckline of her dress, and down over her body and her long, shapely legs to her feet, then back to her face. 'You look stunning.' His eyes, gleaming with all-male appreciation, caught and held hers.

'Thank you,' she murmured, her breath lodged in her throat as she dragged her gaze away from his, and asked in a desperate attempt to free herself from the electrifying sensations he aroused in her and be her usual assertive self, 'I don't know where you planned on eating, but I thought, seeing as you showed me around today, perhaps you would like to be my guest for dinner, in the hotel.'

His firm lips quirked in a crooked smile. 'Call me old-fashioned,' he reached out and cupped her elbow with his hand, 'but when I ask a lady out to dine I make the arrangements, and I'm sure you won't be disappointed,' he said, amusement colouring his tone, and, dropping his hand from her elbow to circle her waist, he held her to his side and turned towards the exit, taking control.

He felt her slender body tremble and stiffen and glanced knowingly down at her. 'I thought we could eat at my villa if you have no objection. Plus you will be doing me a big favour, as my housekeeper loves to cook but I very rarely have any guests to dine when I am here.'

Liza flicked him a bright if strained smile; being held close to his hard body was playing havoc with the cool sophistication she wanted to display. 'Your place is fine,' she agreed. 'So long as the food is not cooked over a volcano like lunch,' she tried to joke. 'It could be dangerous.'

'Good.' Nick dropped his hand and stood back to let her through the foyer door. Nowhere near as dangerous as sharing a suite with your boss, he thought sardonically as he immediately followed her out. The very obliging receptionist had quite happily given him the information. He reached an arm around her shoulders and led her to where the car waited at the kerb, and if his grip was a little hard he had good reason.

Liza felt the touch of his fingers, and repressed a sensual shiver. Nick was a very tactile man, and it was playing hell with her hormones, she thought as a wave of heat scorched her face, but that was all it was—sexual attraction—on her part. That was all it could be, a simple feminine reaction to his raw masculine sexuality. 'No Jeep tonight,' she commented, striving for lightness as they crossed the pavement.

'No,' Nick said shortly.

Then she noticed a man get out of the car and grin at them both as he opened the rear door of the car. Liza shot Nick a startled glance. 'A chauffeur.'

'Yes. Tonight I want to relax and enjoy my dinner with a beautiful woman and share a few glasses of champagne in comfort.' No need to mention he had already downed two very large whiskies because of the dilemma she had created in his usually very well-ordered life. 'And don't worry, I think you will love the meal. Greta is the best cook on the island.' He smiled and lifted a hand casually to flick a strand of her hair over her shoulder and his darkening gaze trapped hers.

She swallowed hard and had trouble speaking. 'I'm sure you are right,' she managed, tearing her gaze away from his and stepping towards the car.

Liza slid quickly into the car with more haste than elegance, sinking into a seat that was a lot more comfortable than Nick's Jeep. But when Nick moved in beside her she realised it was also a lot more intimate as a hard masculine thigh pressed against her own, and a long arm was casually flung around her shoulders yet again.

'Nice car,' she mumbled, intensely aware of his leashed strength, the subtle male scent of the man, and wondered for the umpteenth time what she was doing, playing with fire. But she had been doing that all day both physically and metaphorically, she realised with a wry smile.

The villa turned out to be a magnificent building that oozed wealth and elegance. Nick introduced her to a middle-aged couple waiting in the entrance foyer, Greta and Paul. And beyond them she could see a glass wall that opened on to a floodlit swimming pool, she glimpsed tables and chairs and wondered if they were to eat outside. It wasn't that warm.

She lifted her puzzled gaze to Nick. 'Are we eating outside?'

'*Dios!* No.' His ebony brows arched in surprise. 'What you English think is warm we consider winter.' And, taking her arm, he led her through into a massive room. 'This is the main living area, but the dining room is more cosy,' he said softly.

Liza gazed around the vast room as he urged her across it. Soft deep sofas, exquisite antique furniture, glorious paintings on the walls, and vibrant flowers and plants—the place screamed money, and she was rapidly beginning to feel out of her depth.

Nick pushed open another door, and Liza stopped dead one foot inside the room.

A magnificent table about twenty feet long was set for two, and Greta and Paul were now standing by the table, smiling.

'I'd hardly call this cosy!' she exclaimed with a chuckle. 'You could serve the Last Supper at that table and then some.'

Nick's mouth quirked at the corners in a grin at Liza's stunned expression, and, slipping his arm around her waist, he led her forward. 'I suppose it is a bit imposing; I hadn't really noticed as I usually eat in the kitchen.' He gave her waist a brief squeeze before setting her free, but stayed close to her side. He heard her breath catch and saw the deepening colour in her brilliant eyes, and allowed a small, satisfied smile to curve his lips before adding, 'But I so rarely have anyone to dine here that Greta wanted to push the boat out, as you say.'

Nick leant over slightly to say something to the other couple that Liza, although she spoke Spanish, didn't catch. She watched as they left the room then Nick straightened up to his full, impressive height, and turned to face her again, pulling out a chair.

'Please, Liza, sit down, and don't look so wary; I can assure you, Paul and Greta won't poison you.'

It wasn't the food Liza was worried about; it was much too hot in here, she told herself, and it had absolutely nothing to do with Nick. She reached for the edge of her shawl, and immediately Nick's hand caught it and slipped it off her shoulders.

'A little warm for you, Liza?' he queried with the arch of a black brow.

'Yes,' she got out, having difficulty breathing as the backs of his knuckles brushed down over her breasts as he removed her shawl, but not by the blink of an eye did she let it show. Instead she sat down on the chair he offered and folded her hands primly in her lap, her fingernails digging into her palms.

Liza wasn't afraid to be alone with Nick—in fact, if she was honest she liked the idea. She had enjoyed his company all day, more so than that of any other man she had ever met, and she was secretly flattered that he wanted to be alone with her.

'Now, isn't this nice?' Nick remarked, pulling out a chair and sitting down. 'So much more intimate than a restaurant, don't you think?' Shovelling on the charm by the bucket-load, he picked up the linen napkin in front of her and flicked it open.

'I can do that.' She reached for the linen.

'But I want to,' Nick said softly and, leaning forward, his dark eyes holding her startled blue, he spread the linen napkin over her lap, his hands deliberately smoothing the fabric over her stomach and thighs. 'Greta is going to serve the meal in a minute.' His glance roamed over her face and figure with obvious male approval that, had it been any other man, would have made her angry, but instead the lingering touch of his fingers on her thighs made her whole body tingle with excitement.

'I am hungry, and I'm sure you are too,' Nick drawled with silken emphasis.

She tensed at the impact of his compelling dark gaze. Was it just food he was hungry for? Dear heaven, her own appetite had been seriously depleted by the erotic thoughts Nick aroused in her. She felt as if a thousand butterflies were partying in her stomach, and she tore her eyes away from his and cast a slightly panicked look around the room.

What were her options? Get up and walk out? But that would be childish. Or stay and eat like a civilised woman? Suddenly she was no longer feeling quite so confident. But her mind was made up for her as Greta reappeared carrying a large silver tureen, followed by Paul carrying a bottle of champagne in a silver wine bucket. They both smiled at her.

CHAPTER THREE

THE champagne cork popped and Liza jumped, and then grinned. She was overreacting—everything was perfect. Nick was seated at the head of the table and Paul was filling crystal flutes with very expensive champagne, and Greta was serving a delicious fish soup into the finest porcelain bowls.

When they had both left Nick picked up his glass, and said, 'Here's to you, Liza, and a pleasant evening, for both of us.'

She managed to control the slight nervousness that assailed her when they were alone, and she lifted her glass. 'I'll drink to that.' Her steady voice and hand gratified her no end as they touched glasses.

Nick grinned and swirled the liquid around in his glass, then lifted it to his lips and swallowed before returning the glass to the table.

Liza followed the movement, her gaze stopping at his perfectly sculptured mouth, and she was helpless against the flush of heat that flooded her body as he took a deep drink of the champagne. Realising she was staring, she took a hasty drink from her glass. 'Lovely champagne,' she enthused. And saw him nod, his dark eyes lifting to hers.

'Lovely companion.' He touched his glass to hers again and then added, 'And I am glad you agreed to dining here, Liza. Restaurants can be so impersonal sometimes, and I really want to talk to you, reminisce, and perhaps discover what has shaped you into the very lovely lady you are today.' His glance dropped from her face to the firm curves of her breasts, and she felt them tighten alarmingly against

38

the silk fabric of her dress. 'Get to know the real you again.'

'That sounds ominous,' she offered and, dropping her head, praying he would not notice her body's instant reaction, she added, 'You might not like the real me,' and carefully placed her glass on the table. Quickly she picked up a spoon and began shovelling the soup into her mouth. When she dared look up again, she needed not have worried.

'Impossible. I already adore you, as you know; I have since you were a child,' he said smoothly, his expression wryly amused. 'Now, let us enjoy our meal, and you can tell me what you have been doing with your life over the past few years.' His smile was irresistible.

'Not a lot.' Flattered, Liza grinned back. 'And certainly nothing exciting enough to need privacy before disclosure.' And she proceeded to give him a potted history of her adult life. 'Three years in university reading history, and a job I enjoy, as I told you before. I have a studio apartment in London and I visit my mother every few weeks. She got married again three years ago and lives in Brighton, running an antique shop with Jeff, my stepfather. These are hardly state secrets.'

'Oh, I don't know,' Nick responded with a devilish gleam in his dark eyes. 'You might have become a porn star or a lap dancer; you certainly have the figure for it. And then there are your lovers. You have a high-powered job so maybe a lover or two in high places as well?'

His sexy teasing brought an embarrassing tinge of pink to her cheeks. Was he insinuating that was all she was good for, as he had years ago? Liza wondered, but refused to rise to the bait. 'You know what I do for a living.' She held his gaze. 'But as for the rest, that *is* classified information,' she managed to respond archly, much to her satisfaction.

Nick just bet it was. She was either very clever or very naive, and Liza looked far too sophisticated to be naive.

He could not decide if she was completely in the know about her boss's alternative career as a diamond smuggler or not, but for Carl's sake he was taking no chances.

One eyebrow rose eloquently. 'Of course, I expected no less, Liza.' And the sardonic glance he cast her was oddly intent. 'Though I have heard Henry Brown is not quite so reticent in his love life, although he is married, I believe.'

For a moment something unsettling about his comment teased at the back of her mind. But, dismissing the errant thought, she responded drily, 'Henry is a law unto himself where women are concerned. And, though personally I deplore unfaithfulness in a marriage, I must admit, having met his wife, I'm not surprised.' She tried for a sophisticated answer. Plus Margot Brown was a pretentious snob; the few times she visited the office or spoke to Liza or any of the staff she treated them as if they were a sub-species.

'I believe you; after all, it must be great to have a boss who books a suite at a five-star hotel to attend a conference then quite happily takes off and gives you a holiday with all expenses paid at the drop of a hat. I must confess I am nowhere near as generous with my employees,' Nick drawled sardonically.

Liza looked up sharply. What was he implying? And she answered her own question. She wasn't a fool, she could tell when she was being insulted, and the old hurt resurfaced, causing a brief stabbing pain in her heart. Obviously he still thought of her as a promiscuous teenager and her blue eyes glinted with anger at the injustice of it all. 'It is a two-bedroom suite.' She held on to her temper with difficulty, determined not to show any emotion over the past in front of him. 'And my boss was called away unexpectedly.' Straightening in her seat, she added with contrived flippancy, 'So who am I to argue? You know the saying, never look a gift-horse in the mouth.'

'Yes.' He did, but at the mention of 'mouth' Nick found his eyes fixed on the very generous curve of Liza's, and imagined nibbling that full bottom lip... *Dios!* He had to stop these thoughts. He never mixed business with pleasure. But then he had never been confronted by the adult Liza before.

Dropping his gaze to the less tempting table, he continued in a softer tone, 'I suppose you are right, Liza. But isn't it rather odd that he does not want you to attend the meetings?'

'I…well…' Liza hesitated; his quite reasonable question made her think and defused her anger. She supposed it was a bit unusual.

'I really don't know.' She told the truth. 'I have only been his PA for a couple of months; his last one left to get married, and, as my boss retired about the same time, Henry sort of inherited me,' she explained, not sure why she was bothering. 'This is the first time I have travelled with him. And he is returning a week next Friday for the last day and the gala dinner in the evening, so maybe it will not be a complete waste.'

'I hope not.' Nick had the information he required and a flash of triumph glinted in his dark eyes; the man was coming back to the island in thirteen days' time. The time span was about right for the negotiations; obviously Brown was returning to collect the money and he was as good as caught. A call to Carl, and, with the other culprits tracked down hopefully by the Spanish police and Interpol, the arrests were a foregone conclusion.

'Yes, and we are returning to London together the next day, as scheduled,' Liza added.

Not if he could help it, was Nick's immediate thought. Liza had said she had only been Brown's PA for a short time; that was easily checked and if true was in Liza's favour. She could be innocent. His dark eyes narrowed assessingly on her apparently guileless face. A woman could look beautiful and innocent and still be a criminal. He was not foolish enough to think otherwise, and yet he knew he didn't want Liza anywhere near Henry Brown when they picked him up.

At the very least she would end up being taken in for questioning, and that he could not allow. Surprisingly for him, he discovered he was not ready to part with Liza now he had met up with her again. At his age and with his experience of women, he knew the feeling for what it was—lust, stark and basic...

Liza had been an itch he could not scratch for years when she was younger, but not any more. He wanted to sate himself in that gorgeous body until she was out from under his skin for good.

Nick lifted the champagne flute and took a sip of the wine, then twirled the stemmed glass in his long fingers, studying the colour for several seconds, thinking quickly. Finally he shifted his dark gaze to linger appreciatively on her.

'Your boss is a very lucky man,' he declared huskily, his firm lips curving in a soft, sensual smile, 'to have you as his PA.' Little did Brown know, his luck had just about run out, Nick thought with savage satisfaction even as he mouthed the slick compliment.

'Thanks,' she said drily. But felt the colour rise in her cheeks as her eyes met his, too conscious of his virile charm and something in his expression that made her heartbeat increase dramatically. She finished her soup to hide her confusion, and was grateful when Greta reappeared with the next course.

As Nick had promised, the food was beautiful, and as they ate Nick took charge of the conversation and Liza was happy to follow. They talked in an easy manner, discussing films, books, music, and Nick's experiences on various projects. Liza was fascinated and asked dozens of questions. He told her how he had expanded the company worldwide. He spoke with dry humour of the different business practices in the different countries, and the amusing situations that arose from the differences.

Nick was not the wealthy, idle lotus-eater she had thought; he obviously worked hard. But his skill, his charm, was such that he made everything appear easy. He told a good story, sometimes against himself, but she formed the impression that whatever the circumstances Nick always came out the winner. He had a brilliant mind, and she doubted anyone crossed him and got away with it.

Scraping the last mouthful of the mouth-watering soufflé into her mouth, she glanced up at him through the thick fringe of her lashes. 'In a way you and I are a bit alike— you studied art and don't use it. I read history at university and thought I would visit all the great historical places in the world, but instead I have ended up in finance, a bit of a waste.'

'The experience of university life is an end in itself,' Nick argued. 'And I do use my knowledge; I appreciate anything of beauty, be it a woman or a landscape, I know where to site a building so it is aesthetically pleasing, though, with the upsurge in tourism around here in the last few years, some are anything but.'

Liza chuckled. 'I never thought of that.'

'Have you ever thought of changing, Liza?' Nick demanded seriously. 'You're young—you have plenty of time to start another career.' He was satisfied he had discovered all he needed to know. Henry Brown was returning to Lanzarote. As for Liza, he was almost sure she was innocent of any crime, and, even if she was guilty, once away from financial temptation and into something more academic it was possible she could change, and he never questioned his reasoning, simply pursued the thought.

'You could get out of finance and back into what you really want to do,' he suggested. 'It is never too late, Liza, believe me. I might even be able to help you.'

'I suppose you're right.' Liza smiled. 'But don't take it so seriously, Nick; I'll survive whatever.' And she sat back with a sigh of contentment. 'That meal was magnificent, Greta is a great cook.'

'You can tell her that in a minute,' Nick said curtly. He didn't know why but her casual attitude infuriated him, had she no idea of the danger she was in? Did she even care? Pushing back his chair, he stood up. 'Greta will serve coffee in the sitting room.'

But what was really bugging him was his superior intellect had apparently deserted him. He had already missed half of the family celebration in Spain and if he didn't get back to his mother's for the final party he and his mother were hosting tomorrow evening, his mother would never forgive him. But what to do with Liza? He dared not leave her alone on the island without telling Carl or he would never forgive him either.

He had been racking his brains to think of some way of persuading Liza to come to Spain with him, and incidentally keep her out of harm's way, but was damned if he knew how to do it. Short of asking her 'Will you come to Spain with me for the rest of the weekend?' But he knew that would go down like a lead balloon, given that she had made a point of avoiding visiting the Menendez home for years.

No, he had to think of something else, and, confident as he was in his masculine powers of seduction, he doubted all the seductive technique in the world would convince Liza to fly off to Spain with him only a day after their meeting up again.

Rising to her feet, Liza followed him through into the elegant living room, wondering what had caused the sudden coolness in the atmosphere. She sat down on one of the soft hide sofas, the occasional table already held the accompaniments for coffee, and a moment later Greta appeared with a pot to add to the already prepared tray.

Liza smiled at the other woman and thanked her for a lovely meal, and then stiffened when Nick chose to sit down beside her on the sofa instead of taking the one opposite. During the meal there had been space between them and the atmosphere had been good most of the time, but now she sensed a tension in the air, and she felt distinctly crowded.

'Will you be mother?' Nick asked smoothly.

The words hung in the air as Liza had a vivid mental image of being mother to Nick's child, a small dark-haired angel. Her face turned scarlet at the provocative thought and hastily she bent forward and filled two small cups with the aromatic coffee. 'Sugar, milk?' she asked, without looking at him.

'As it comes.'

Lifting one cup, she turned slightly, her hand stilling. Nick was lounging back against the cushions, one long arm flung along the back, his jacket hanging open and his shirt pulled tight across his muscular chest, she could see the slight shading of body hair and swallowed hard.

He gave her a long, sardonic look. 'Are you going to give me the coffee, or simply hold it?'

Blushing at her stupidity—she was eyeing the man like the dumb teenager she had once been—she thrust the cup at him, a little of the liquid spilling, and his long fingers curved around hers.

'Steady, Liza. I want to drink it, not drown in it,' he drawled mockingly.

The touch of his hand sent a warmth shimmering through her, and quickly she snatched her hand back, and, grasping her own cup of coffee, forced herself to sit back against the sofa, and lift the cup to her mouth. She took one sip and almost burnt her tongue. Her lips tightened and she just prevented a yelp escaping.

She had to get over her panic; hadn't she decided in the hotel earlier to take a chance? Nick was just a man like any other. But that was the trouble, he was not like any other man she had ever known, she thought ruefully, casting him a sidelong glance from beneath the thick screen of her lashes. How was it, she mused, that as a young girl she had had a crush on him and was brutally cured of the illusion by the man himself? For years she thought she hated him and yet now one day in his company and all she saw was a dominant, attractive male who turned her bones to jelly.

Feeling vulnerable in a man's presence for the first time in years, she was not sure she trusted the feeling, and common sense told her to thank Nick for the meal and leave. With that in mind she drained her coffee-cup and replaced it on the table, and, turning slightly, she glanced at his face. He was looking down at her, his mouth a hard, taut line, and for a moment Liza felt a slight shiver of fear, or was it a shiver of sensual anticipation? She was not sure which, and quickly fixed her gaze somewhere over his left shoulder and before she could weaken.

'Thank you for a lovely evening, Nick. But I think it is time I got back to my hotel.' She made to rise, only to find a large restraining hand on her forearm.

'Please join me in a brandy at least,' Nick said softly, and placed his cup on the table, his dark gaze holding her own, and his thumb caressing the underside of her arm to devastating effect.

Liza was in two minds when the arrival of Paul solved the problem for her.

'Your mother is on the line.' He addressed Nick, a cordless telephone in his hand.

Saved by the bell! Nick thought, a huge smile lighting his handsome features, and took the telephone. 'Hi, Mamma.' He listened with delight as she harangued him about leaving her a note, and flying off to Lanzarote when she had been expecting him at home.

'You were supposed to join your uncle and family tonight for dinner, and you'd better get yourself back here quick for the celebratory lunch and the party tomorrow night.'

'Yes, I will be there, I promise. In fact I will leave tonight, to make absolutely sure, don't worry.'

Listening to the one-sided conversation, Liza berated herself for her stupid fear five minutes ago, and her clumsy attempt to leave. Nick had plans for the rest of the weekend and the dinner was just as he had said. Two old friends catching up with each other. Then she heard the rest…

'But you will never guess who I bumped into today.' Nick shot Liza a brief grin and added, 'Liza, Liza Summers; she is on holiday here, and we've just had dinner together.'

As Nick knew she would, his mother responded, 'Oh, I haven't seen Liza in years. Perhaps you can bring Liza back with you for the party. I would love to meet her again.'

'Well, why don't you ask her yourself, Mamma?' Nick relaxed back against the cushions, ignoring Liza's frantic shaking of her head, and held out the telephone to her while tightening his grip on her arm. 'Mother would like to speak to you, Liza.'

Reluctantly Liza accepted the telephone. Anna Menendez was a very persuasive woman, as her son knew fine well, Liza thought balefully.

'Well, of course I would love to see you again, and it is very kind to invite me, but I really couldn't put Nick to the trouble of flying me to Spain and then back to Lanzarote again.' Five minutes later when she handed the telephone back to Nick she was committed to going to Spain with him.

'I don't believe it.' Liza jumped to her feet. 'Why on earth did you tell your mother I was here?' She glanced down at Nick as he placed the telephone on the table. Call over.

'Because you were,' he said with a shrug of his wide shoulders, and a devilish grin in her direction. Thanks to his mother his problem was solved. Nick had set out this morning with the intention of seducing Liza into giving him the information he wanted, but as the day progressed it was he who had been seduced by Liza's beauty, her warmth, her genuine enthusiasm for life. He would ask her outright about the diamonds in case she had any more information. But he didn't give a damn if she was guilty or not, he was keeping her with him for a few more days and that was all he cared about.

'But you must have known that she'd feel obliged to ask me to her party?'

Rising to his feet, he studied her from beneath lowered lids, the soft, silky skin and the generous curve of her mouth, but at the moment she was bristling with indignation. She knew she had been manipulated—she wasn't stupid. Nick hesitated, a hint of wariness flickering through his eyes.

The mood she was in, if he asked her about the theft of the diamonds, and she was innocent, he could kiss goodbye any chance of getting her into his bed. She would probably never speak to him again, and not surprisingly he found he did not like that idea one bit. He dismissed the thought of challenging her about the diamonds—that could wait. He could sense she was moments away from changing her mind, and he had to do something fast.

'I never thought, but it seems like a good idea.' He reached for her shoulders, and held her gently. 'My mother is not getting any younger and she has been quite down lately; seeing you again is just the tonic she needs to cheer her up—she always had a soft spot for you.' It wasn't a lie; his mother had been down, but a course of antibiotics for a mild chest infection had put her right again, and he saw no need to tell Liza that. Emotional blackmail, sensual persuasion…he utilised all his skills. 'And I am very reluctant to part with you so soon after meeting you again, Liza.' A gentle pressure with his fingers, and a shiver arced down her spine. 'Will it be such a hardship to spend a few days' holiday in Spain and make an old woman happy?'

Hardship, no, but it was likely to cause her enormous pain, resurrecting old memories. Captivated by the sincerity in Nick's dark eyes, she could feel her resentment at his high-handiness weakening. He loved his mother, of that she had no doubt.

'I suppose not.' He sounded perfectly reasonable, and put

like that he was right. But she stiffened in his hold, mortified by her helpless response to his touch. She hated to admit it, but she had read such a lot into her meeting with Nick, the day out and everything, and it was humiliating to realise he hadn't been bowled over by her looks or her personality; in fact, he probably still thought of her as the no-good little tramp of years ago. Nothing had changed...

Nick watched myriad expressions flutter over her exquisite features, and knew she was still not totally convinced, so bending his dark head, he brushed her lips with his own. 'You think too much, Liza.'

'Better than not thinking at all,' Liza shot back sarcastically, but her heart was not in it. She told herself she had fallen for Nick's soft soap like a stupid kid all over again. She should have remembered what an arrogant, conceited swine he was, intent on getting his own way whatever the cost. But somehow, with her lips tingling from the taste of him, however hard she tried she could not sustain her anger with him.

'Relax, Liza, you will enjoy yourself. Come and sit down, have a brandy.'

'I think I need one,' Liza murmured and let him lead her back to the sofa, and made no objection when, seated beside her, he kept one arm around her waist, holding her close to his side.

'You know my mother,' he prompted with a wry smile. 'She gets an idea in her head and won't budge. She still thinks she offended you and that is why you have never visited in years. My jet is standing by at the airport, Liza, you're unexpectedly free for a week or so...there will never be a better time.'

With a flash of insight Liza knew she would let this man take her anywhere; after years of frustration she had finally met again the man whose slightest touch thrilled her to the core. 'I don't have a choice,' she said drily. 'I have already told your mother I would go.' And she had already told herself earlier she wanted to see where the relationship with Nick would lead, and she would never have a better chance.

'Never mind Mamma, I want you to come for me,' Nick husked and looked long and deep into her eyes.

Liza felt as if he was looking into her soul, and what she had thought was a simple case of sexual chemistry between them suddenly took on a frightening dimension. She noted tiny flecks of gold in the darkening depths of his eyes, and all her muscles tensed as she forgot his mother, forgot everything except the heady awareness of this man that filled her mind to the exclusion of everything else.

'Nick,' she thought, not realising she had said his name out loud. He tugged at her heart-strings like no other man before, or ever would again, she realised with blinding clarity. She wanted him, and instinctively she moved closer to his side.

'Yes, Liza.' His voice roughened as he held her firmly then quickly slipped his other arm around her to draw her even closer. She felt the hardness of his body and the heat of him searing her, even through the fabric of her dress. His dark head bent and his lips hovered over hers. 'I knew you would be sensible,' he murmured and then he kissed her, his tongue slipping between her parted lips in a deeply sensual kiss.

This wasn't sensible, Liza knew. He was implying a brief affair, but his mouth was tender and moist, filling her with sensation until she couldn't think. His hand caressed slowly up her side and over the soft mound of one breast, and a tiny moan escaped her. His powerful sexuality overwhelmed her, making the blood run hot through her veins, and she was lost in the wonder of his embrace when he lifted his head and eased back slightly and murmured, 'Think of us, Liza.'

'Us?' She was totally confused.

'Yes,' Nick promised, one hand gently cupping her chin. 'I have to leave tonight.' He kissed her again. 'And I want you with me quite desperately.' He mouthed the words against her lips as his other hand caught hers and pressed it to his hard manhood. 'Feel what you do to me,' he rasped sexily.

Her breath snagged in her throat and she saw his pupils dilating so his eyes were sinful black pools of hunger. She flexed her fingers and heard him groan. She pulled her hand away, afraid she had hurt him. Equally as ravenous for him.

He kissed her again with a deep, possessive passion, and when his mouth lifted from hers Liza's arms were around his neck, and the breath was drawn from her body. She pulled back and briefly closed her eyes, fighting to recover her breath, the longing to know Nick in every way an almost physical pain, and thought, why not?

She might never get another chance to feel the miracle of his lovemaking and she wanted to more than anything else in her life, he had haunted her dreams for years. She was on holiday, and plenty of girls had a holiday romance they remembered with affection after it was over, without ruining their lives…she rationalised. So why not her?

Boldly she curled her arms around his neck again and urged his head down, and kissed him back with a passion, a need she had never imagined she was capable of.

'You are exquisite,' Nick opined huskily and, lifting his dark head, a dull flush along his high cheekbones, he added, 'We will have a wonderful time, trust me,' and immediately felt a twinge of guilt, an alien emotion for him. He had used her obvious attraction to him to get the result that he required, but he had never expected to want Liza quite so badly. 'Hoist by his own petard' sprang to mind…

'I'll keep you to that,' Liza murmured huskily, and, raising brilliant blue eyes, she gulped at the unguarded smouldering desire in the black depths of his, and for a moment her throat closed in panic. Nick was so sure of himself, his sexuality so potent—was she really ready for this? Her one attempt at sex had left her thinking it was vastly overrated or she was frigid.

Nick saw the flash of uncertainty in her glorious eyes,

and, not giving her time to dwell on it, he rose to his feet, taking Liza with him. 'A call to your hotel for your luggage,' he informed her and drew her hard against him, allowing her to feel the extent of his need, and he kissed her once again hard and fast. 'And we can leave within the hour.'

Leave! Hell, he wanted to tumble her down on the sofa and take her now. It was what they had both been fighting all day, or maybe longer…he wasn't sure about anything any more, except the need to get her away from Lanzarote, he reminded himself, and stepped back, setting her free.

Liza blinked and for one wild moment wondered what she had committed to. As he stood before her, dark and slightly dangerous with certain possessiveness in his eyes, she suddenly felt threatened, and she did not understand why.

His request was straightforward enough, and after a few tense seconds she smoothed damp palms down over her hips and said lightly, 'You and your mother seem to have it all arranged, and it will be nice to see Anna again, so far be it from me to disappoint you all.' She could play the sophisticate as good as any woman.

'You could never disappoint me, Liza,' Nick said in a throaty voice, and with a faint smile he slid one long finger down her burning cheek in a tender gesture. 'But if we don't stop this now, I cannot be responsible for my actions,' he said thickly, his finger tracing the outline of her slightly swollen lips.

Helplessly Liza's lips parted and just as abruptly Nick stepped back. 'No.' His great chest heaved. 'Later, or we will never get out of here. I think we need that brandy now.'

CHAPTER FOUR

'Now that wasn't too painful, was it, Liza?' Nick asked, releasing his safety belt, and, turning, he deftly unfastened the belt restraining her in the flight seat next to him, but not before dropping a swift kiss on her full lips. He saw her eyes darken, and it crossed his mind that it was after ten in the evening and there was a bedroom on the plane. It was a two-hour flight, and he doubted if a girl with Liza's obvious sexual appetite would object.

'Painful, no. A mad rush, yes,' Liza quipped, striving for some sense of normality even as her head spun from his brief kiss. 'You do realise we will arrive in Spain in the middle of the night? That is hardly going to go down well with your mother.'

She was still not sure she was doing the right thing. But Nick was very persuasive. As he had said when she was dithering while waiting for the car to take them to the airport, it was only for a few days, and it would mean the world to his mother. Liza recognised it was emotional blackmail but powerful nevertheless.

Nick's comment that they could have fun as well and the sensual gleam in his dark eyes had told her exactly what he meant. When she had queried how she would get back to Lanzarote, he had told her not to worry, he would take care of everything and her boss needed never know she had been away. Which, she thought drily, put it in perspective; a brief affair was all he had in mind, and it was up to her just how much *fun* it would be.

Nick considered her thoughtfully; she was nervous and striving to cover it. He had been keeping up a subtle sensual pressure in case she changed her mind, and would like to think it was his obvious attraction that was making her nervous but he could not suppress the suspicion it was more likely the change in her plans that he had contrived. The cynical side of his nature reminded him that in his experience a really good criminal rarely liked their schedule altered by an outside influence. 'Let me worry about Mamma,' he reassured her with a lazy smile. 'Relax.'

Easy for him to say, but Liza was on her way back to the house where she'd suffered her biggest humiliation, and she was scared. 'Will there be a lot of people at this party?' she asked, lifting guarded blue eyes to his, and there was something about the way he looked at her with a kind of amused sensuality that was incredibly arousing and she could not tear her gaze away.

'Quite a few. You know Mamma; it is her brother and his wife's golden-wedding anniversary.' He was aware that she was staring at him as intently as he was studying her and the amusement vanished from his face as her gaze involuntarily darkened, the tension between them renewing itself with a cosmic force.

How did she do that? Confuse him… One look from her baby blues, and she made him feel guilty for being economical with the truth, and at the same time turned him on so hard his loins ached.

'You worry too much,' he insisted, strain making his tone curt. He leaned back in his seat and circled his shoulders to ease the tension. It had been a horrendously long day; the anger that had sustained him this morning had calmed somewhat after meeting Liza again, and getting the information he required. But he felt as if he had been walking on eggshells for the past few hours. Never forgetting his primary concern was to help Carl catch the criminals, but at the same time endeavouring to protect Liza from the result of her own actions; whether with criminal intent or not, she was involved up to her swan-like neck. But what to do about Liza he still was not sure…

He knew what he wanted to do... She made him feel like a randy teenager again.

He cast a sidelong glance at Liza and he saw the uneven rise and fall of her breasts, the subtle scent of her perfume—or was it simply her—fogged his brain and his body tightened another notch.

Nick dragged an unsteady hand through his hair. They were airborne now; she could not change her mind and getting her out of Lanzarote was for her own good, he told himself. He owed it to the delightful child she had been to protect her. He could not let her go to jail. It should have made him feel better, but it didn't. Instead beneath his cool exterior he was struggling to contain emotions that were as unwelcome as they were unfamiliar.

Had he taken leave of his senses? How the hell was he going to explain to Carl that he had taken off with one of the prime suspects? His friend would think he was crazy. Maybe he was. But he knew he would do anything, pay anything to keep Liza out of trouble with the law, and if that made him a fool, so be it.

Leaping to his feet, he crossed to a cream leather sofa. Slipping off his jacket and tugging his tie loose in the process, he dropped them and his long length down on it, his angry eyes raking over her. Frustration wasn't the word!

Liza was a walking, talking sex goddess. Either in trousers and a cheap top with her glorious hair scraped back in a childish pony-tail, as he had seen her this morning, or with her hair a tumbled mass around her shoulders and elegant in black wrap-around dress that was just begging to be unwrapped. Crook or not, she turned him on without even trying.

'To hell with it!' he swore under his breath. Keeping her out of jail did not mean he had to keep her out of his bed. She had matured into an incredibly sexy, sophisticated lady, and he was acting like an idiot. He was a man who prided himself on his control and anger bubbled beneath the sur-

face of his smooth smile as he gestured with one hand to
the adjoining sofa.

'Take a softer seat. You'll be more comfortable,' he offered, and watched as she rose from the aircraft seat, her
hands nervously sweeping the smooth fabric of her dress
over her hips, and he almost groaned out loud.

She looked so shy, almost innocent, and that was part of
her charm, or her act, he reminded himself cynically, and,
unfolding his long length from the sofa, he stepped towards
her. 'But perhaps a guided tour first,' he suggested, curving
his hand over her shoulder. 'The plane is divided into three
compartments—this seating area, a bedroom and restroom.'

Liza had never seen anything like it. How the other half
lives, she thought drily, but it was luxury with a capital L.
Soft leather sofas and chairs, an occasional table and thick
cream carpet, a bar in one corner, near a door that led to
the galley and to the flight deck. Nick had introduced her
to the captain and crew when they boarded. At the opposite
end towards the rear of the aircraft was a corridor with a
couple more doors leading off. She knew people who lived
in smaller apartments than this plane; the thought made her
smile.

'It all looks very luxurious and very expensive.' She
lifted sparkling blue eyes to his. 'It must be great to be so
rich you can have your own aircraft.'

The smile in her eyes took his breath away. But her
comment also made him wonder if she was greedy for
money. Thief, gold-digger, he didn't give a damn.

'It has its compensations.' Nick's voice roughened as he
turned her into his arms, and did what he had been aching
to do since they left the villa. He ran his hands down the
shapely length of her supple body, felt her tremble and then
crushed her ruthlessly against the hard heat of his own.
Using his innate masculine ability to arouse her, he quite
deliberately lowered his head and brushed her pouting lips
with his.

She was sweet, so sweet… He tasted her with lips and tongue, savouring her like a connoisseur of fine wine, and then he deepened the kiss until he felt her slender arms wrap around his neck. He lifted his head, the briefest of triumphant smiles curling his hard mouth, and, drawing a deep, rasping breath, he took a chance. 'Let me show you.' He didn't add 'the bedroom'; he didn't need to.

Liza didn't know what hit her—one minute she was talking to him, and the next she was enfolded in Nick's arms. The mere touch of him had turned her legs to water, and when he kissed her a surge of heat enveloped her whole body. She clung to him, and when he smiled at her she began to tremble as she gazed at him in mesmerised fascination.

He was incredibly handsome with the most gorgeous, slumberous, come-to-bed eyes, dark as night and yet with a sensual gleam as gold as the rising sun. He had to be over six feet four, he was the only man she had ever met she really had to look up to. Her mouth ran dry and she felt a sudden heaviness in her breasts as her nipples tightened in helpless response.

Show her what? The thought crossed her mind but was lost as one long finger traced the outline of her full lips, then moved along her jawline to curve around her ear. She involuntarily swayed into him as his large hand moved swiftly on to the nape of her neck, his long fingers burrowing under the heavy fall of her hair. His hand was smooth but she was intensely aware of the strength in his grip, and for a second she stiffened in apprehension.

But then he lowered his head once more, and his mouth traced the curve of her cheek, tantalisingly close to her. Heat kindled in the pit of her stomach, and she couldn't think straight, didn't try… This was what she wanted, what she yearned for, and she turned her head slightly to find his teasing lips with her own.

A wild recklessness swept through her as his mouth took

hers with a ruthless, demanding passion that in seconds had her on fire. Her slender fingers tangled through his silky black hair as his tongue delved deep, and she welcomed the hard, savage mouth, gloried in the meeting. They kissed with a ferocious hunger that emptied her head of everything but a growing deep physical ache that curled and tightened in the centre of her body.

Suddenly she was swept up in his arms, and her head fell back as his tongue licked down every inch of her throat to the shadow between her breasts. Liza closed her eyes and felt her whole body melting bonelessly in his arms, and then slowly he raised his head.

'Look at me,' Nick demanded. 'Is this what you want, Liza?' he asked in a deep slightly accented drawl.

Her dazed blue eyes clashed with jet black, and for a second she saw a look of such predatory hunger in his expression some tiny corner of her mind tried to warn her to be wary. She dragged in a ragged breath, trying to fight the pull of his attraction. 'The steward,' she murmured inanely. He had asked earlier if they wanted a drink and Nick had dismissed him, but…

'It is more than his job's worth.' Nick declared with arrogant certainty, but the slight colour tracing his high cheekbones and the clenching of his fingers in her hair told her he was no less affected by the desire flooding through them than she was. Her pupils dilated to almost obscure the blue, she opened her mouth to reply, but, reading the answer in her eyes, he did not wait.

He shouldered the door open and in two strides he lowered her down onto the large bed. Discarding his shirt, his great body looming over her, he reached down and untied the knot at her waist and peeled her dress open.

Liza should have been shy, exposed in only black lace briefs, but her eyes widened on his lean, strong face, her pulse racing as she checked down to the broad shoulders. All her attention was captured by the perfection of his tanned, muscular chest, the intriguing pattern of black curling body hair that arrowed down to where his trousers hung low on his hips. He was her dream come true, she had waited what felt like a lifetime for this man, and at last she was trembling on the brink of knowing the full wonder of Nick, her heart's secret desire.

'You are exquisite,' Nick growled, his gaze roaming over her near-naked length, before he sank down beside her, and ran his long fingers through the silken mass of her hair. He then trailed one long strand with teasing expertise over a firm breast, a rosy tip, and watched her nipple tighten, saw her body arch in an involuntary motion she could not hide. He surveyed her hungrily. 'Ravishing...' and that was exactly what he intended doing to her...

Hypnotised by his slow, sensual exploration, Liza caught her breath as he reached for her. Stripping her dress from her shoulders, his hands were everywhere. One skimming over her breasts, the other tracing the length of her leg from knee to thigh, while with lips and tongue he tormented her with kisses and tantalising caresses over her face and throat.

'So are you,' she breathed, so caught up in the excitement, the pleasure he aroused, she was scarcely aware of what she was saying. Long fingers traced her inner thigh, and brushed against the scrap of black lace. Liza groaned out loud, as at the same time his teeth found a dusky nipple and teased with tiny bites.

Unbelievable sensations arrowed through her body as he began to suckle before he turned his attentions to the other rigid peak. He didn't hurry, he suckled and licked, and at the same time his seeking fingers slipped beneath the black lace and stroked the hot wet centre of her femininity. Her eyes widened in shocked pleasure before he took her lips in a brief, hard kiss, and continued his tantalising exploration of every inch of her until she was writhing on the bed like a woman possessed.

Liza grasped his broad shoulders with both hands, shaped

them, loving the feel of sleek, satin skin. Then, with an innate sensuality she did not know she possessed, ran her hands down over his chest, discovering the massive breadth, the hard male nipples in the silken whorls of chest hair, her fingers tracing the ridges of perfectly defined muscles. Daringly she dipped lower until she fumbled with the button of his trousers. Nick helped her and obligingly slid off his trousers and boxers.

Incredibly for a girl who had thought she did not like sex, thought she was frigid, Liza couldn't stop her fingers from trailing the long, hard length of his erection, curving her slender fingers around him. She had never realised how much she had been missing; his body was beautiful, a tactile feast of epic proportions.

'No.' His hoarsely groaned command and his hand capturing hers stopped her frenzied exploration. 'Slowly, Liza, slowly.' She heard the sharp intake of his breath as their mouths met.

She wasn't really conscious of him removing her briefs as desire mounted frantically inside her, driving everything else from her mind, except for the burning need to have Nick there…where the heat was most intense…

He moved over her and she felt the roughness of his chest against her sensitised nipples. Then his mouth invaded hers yet again, the kiss replicating what she ached for him to do with his body. She wrapped her arms around his broad back and traced the length of his spine, her small hand curving around his hard buttock, her fingers digging into his flesh.

Liza felt his heart pounding into her almost painfully but she exalted in the feeling, his passion consuming her, and she abandoned herself to the driving hunger that had her in its grip. Her tongue duelled with his, her teeth were creating their own havoc on his lips. But suddenly he reared back, and her arms fell to her sides. 'Nick,' she moaned his name, 'I want you.'

Nick felt the tremble in her body, the hot, wet heat of her, and heard the husky words emerging from her mouth. Unbearably aroused, he feasted his eyes on her, her hair spread out like a pale cloud across the cover, her dazzling blue eyes dazed with desire, the full, firm, rigid-tipped breasts, her skin as smooth as silk, the exquisite body spread beneath him. He had never seen anything so beautiful, and she wanted him.

Nick swallowed a pained groan... Now she told him, when he needed no encouragement! Quite the reverse. He reached over to a drawer by the bed and withdrew a condom. Swiftly in one fluid movement he knelt between her legs, not trying to hide his fierce arousal, and nudged her thighs apart, his thumbs rubbing over the velvet lips, and Liza stretched out her arms to him. He gloried in watching her mindless, breathless and needy, oh, so needy, exactly how he wanted her, but his moment of triumph was short-lived.

Nick could feel his control slipping away as her slender fingers raked down his chest; she was wild and wanton and he was closer to losing it than he had ever been in his life. 'This time I'd better do the honours, or I won't make it,' he rasped.

'Please,' Liza groaned.

Please her he would, Nick vowed, and dipped his dark head and brushed his lips against the soft velvet flesh of her inner thigh, even as his hands touched her, stroked her, squeezed her breasts, driving her ever higher. He was wet with sweat, his muscles trembling, and the scent of her, the feel of her was driving him wild, but still he held back. He had the skill to drive a woman mindless and he utilised every atom he possessed to do just that.

She tensed as his mouth found her, and then she instinctively arched against him, her whole body pulsating with need, every nerve taut, craving for release, spiralling out of control. 'Nick...Nick. Now,' she cried out.

Nick reared up and looked at her with hot black eyes, then slid his hands around her bottom and joined them savagely together with one mighty thrust. Liza gasped, a slight cry escaping her. Nick hesitated, but with barely a pause she wrapped her legs around his waist, urging him on. Her slender body responded to the thrusting hardness of his possession as he moved again and again, deeper and deeper. She was so tight and as the pulsating start of her climax gripped him with a fierce, almost excruciating pleasure he lost it, he had to let go. Together they climaxed in a cataclysmic explosion of raw, primeval passion.

Liza lay still, her slender body hot, damp and totally replete, her arms around Nick, holding him close. His great body pinned her to the bed, but she didn't feel his weight, only an incredible possessive thrill that he was hers at last.

Nothing had prepared her for the wild, primitive passion he aroused in her. She had never realised, never even guessed at the depths of emotion possible between two people. Moisture hazed her eyes, but they were tears of happiness. At last she knew what it was like to be totally possessed by the man who had filled her every erotic thought from puberty, and the beauty, the magic of it was beyond words. How had she ever imagined she hated him?

She took a deep, contented breath and ran slender fingers gently through the damp strands of his curling black hair. He was hers now, and she listened to the ragged sound of his breathing with a fierce joy. She, Liza Summers, the frigid one, had done this to him and her swollen lips curved in a smile so feline she almost purred...

Nick turned his head, saw her smile and pressed a swift kiss to her cheek. 'I'm too heavy for you.' Leaning up on one elbow, he looked down at her.

'No, you're perfect for me,' she murmured. She could see the gleam of masculine satisfaction in his eyes and the hint of a smug grin. 'Perfect,' she reiterated, brimming over with happiness. Her teenage dreams had not begun to touch on the awesome reality of Nick as a lover.

'Glad you approved.' Nick chuckled. 'But I don't want to crush you.' And one elegant hand reached across her slender body to cup her breast, his thumb lazily stroking the tip. 'There are much more interesting things to do with this exquisite body.' He trailed his hand down over her stomach. 'And I intend to explore them all.'

To her amazement her body stirred in response, her breast swelling. She opened her mouth to remark on the astonishing fact and stopped. Nick looked gorgeous, his black hair tousled and his incredible eyes...

'I think I always knew the skinny, coltish teenager would eventually develop the body to tempt a saint.'

Liza blinked and looked again...reality clicking in.

His words had been addressed to her body, not her face, and her brief moment of euphoria was deflated like a burst balloon. He was studying her naked figure like an artist might study a statue. But then why wouldn't he? she reminded herself. He was an expert and his women were legendary, and he was certainly no saint...

She felt the colour surge in her cheeks, and her lashes fluttered down to conceal the pain in her eyes.

'Liza.' She opened her eyes; his face was close and shadowed with stubble, and she had an overwhelming urge to reach up and touch him. 'You OK?' His hand moved from her stomach to twine his fingers in a few long strands of hair. 'You're sure?' He tugged on the lock of hair, his dark eyes narrowing intently on her face.

Amazingly Nick saw she was blushing. Yet she had been everything he imagined and more, wild and willing, he'd never known a woman so responsive. Thinking back, he recalled her shock when he first touched her intimately, her brief flinch, and her slight tensing at times. Perhaps she was not such a promiscuous lady as he had thought. Unless he was very much mistaken it was some time since she'd had a lover and even then not a very expert one if her surprise was anything to go by.

Embarrassed by his analytical scrutiny Liza sat up. 'Never better,' she said brightly, and she gave in to the temptation and lifted her hand and stroked the roughened skin of his jaw. Realising what she was doing, she jerked her hand away and, pulling on the mantle of a sophisticated lady, she added, 'But isn't it time we got dressed?'

She was suddenly very conscious of her nudity, and his, and she was terribly afraid if she didn't put some space between them quickly she might reveal that what for Nick was simply sex between two consenting adults had meant a whole lot more to her. She had never dreamt that she could feel such an intensity of emotion, such passion. In fact after her only other sexual encounter with a man, her ex-fiancé, she had convinced herself great passion was a myth for a woman. Liza felt the prick of tears at the backs of her eyes. How wrong could one get? she thought sadly.

Nick glanced at his wrist-watch, the only thing he was wearing, and groaned. 'You're right, Liza,' he agreed, slanting her a grin. The flush had gone from her face, and her eyes were a little too bright, her smile a little too brittle—not the usual response he got from his women in the afterglow of sex. But he was sure she had enjoyed it as much as he had.

But it was the middle of the night, he rationalised, and, swiftly bending his head, he captured her mouth in a brief, gentle kiss. 'You look tired. I'll take the shower first. I would suggest you join me, but that delight we will have to save for later, or we will never get off the damn plane, and by my reckoning we'll land in twenty minutes.'

Liza watched wide-eyed, she couldn't help herself, as he flung his long legs over the side of the bed and, gloriously unconscious of his nudity, in a few lithe strides he crossed to the far side of the room and disappeared through another door. Moments later she heard the sound of running water, and in her mind's eye she saw his magnificent tanned body, the washboard belly, the hard, lean buttocks, and with a shake of her head she jumped off the bed, and began gathering up her clothes.

So she had had sex with Nick; she must remember sex was all it was...she muttered over and over in her head. A short holiday to attend the party of her mother's friend. Any involvement with Nick had to be light-hearted fun... She could handle it...

CHAPTER FIVE

THE headlights of the car swept over the stable block, and Liza suppressed a tiny shiver of revulsion. Old memories she could do without… Instead she recalled the wonder of feeling the length of Nick's naked body against the heated eagerness of her own, and longed to repeat the experience with a hunger that made her stomach clench. If she closed her eyes she could see the image of their bodies entwined, see the burning desire in his eyes as he captured her mouth in a deeply passionate kiss.

Stifling a groan, she shook her head to chase away the erotic thoughts. The car was moving through a large stone arch and into the rear courtyard of the Menendez Hacienda and Nick brought it to a silent stop outside a large oak door.

Liza scrambled out of the car and, standing up straight, she stretched her shoulders back; she was stiff, tired and suddenly incredibly nervous. Her last visit to this house had been a disaster. What on earth had possessed her to come back? A glance at Nick walking around the front of the car towards her, and she had her answer…

'Are you sure we are expected so late?' she asked with her gaze raking along the long building before them. There appeared to be only a chink of light from beneath what she knew was the rear lobby leading into the large kitchen in the west wing of the hacienda.

'And why the kitchen entrance? Trying to smuggle me in like a thief in the night?' she teased, turning to look at Nick as with one long, easy stride he stood in front of her. She paused, feeling the tension coming from him in a slight hardening of his jawline, a flicker of something she didn't recognise in the depths of his enigmatic eyes. As she saw

66

him outlined in the moon's silver light, the power of his
superbly masculine frame and the inescapable pressure of
the fingertip he lifted to her chin made her shiver in instinc-
tive response.

Damn her! She wasn't far wrong, Nick thought grimly.
He did have an ulterior motive, and even with the unexpected help of his mother he knew it would not take much
to arouse Liza's suspicions. But it also reminded him he
had been so caught up in the witch's spell he had forgotten
to pass on the information to Carl about Brown's return,
and, appalled at his own lapse in concentration on the crime
he was investigating, he lashed out at her.

'And are you a thief?' he demanded curtly, and immediately wished the words unsaid as he saw the humour
flicker and fade from her expressive eyes to be replaced
with a wary puzzlement. 'No, of course not.' He answered
his own question, his mouth curved, as if her comment had
amused him. He did not want her getting suspicious of his
motive, not now… 'Except perhaps of hearts,' he quipped
in a damage-limitation exercise, and, tipping her chin a little higher, he pressed a swift kiss to her softly parted lips,
before reaching for her hand and leading her towards the
door.

'Mamma arranged for Manuel to wait up for us, hence
the back door; you remember him and how he loves to sit
and watch the television in the kitchen.'

Liza did remember, and she accepted his explanation, but
she couldn't dismiss the unsettling notion from her mind
that he had not been joking when he asked her if she was
a thief. She was being ridiculous…it was the middle of the
night…she was having spooky thoughts…

A stream of light suddenly bathed the yard as Manuel
appeared, and when he smiled and said her name with obvious pleasure Liza was touched that he had remembered
her. But in the next minute she was horribly embarrassed
as she heard Nick quite casually tell Manuel to take her
luggage to his room.

Grabbing Nick's sleeve, Liza pulled him back as he would have stridden along the corridor after Manuel. 'Wait a minute,' she spat.

Nick stopped. 'No need to whisper, Liza. There is no one in this wing of the house to hear you, only Manuel, and his wife Marta, who has long since gone to bed,' he drawled, his dark eyes lit with amusement at the furtive look on her lovely face.

'It's not that,' Liza muttered, feeling embarrassed and angry. 'Surely you realise I can't share a room with you in your mother's house.'

His ebony brows rose as he bit out an expletive in Spanish followed by, 'Damn it to hell!' How had he overlooked what he now realised was glaringly obvious? He had leapt at the chance to use his mother's telephone call to get Liza off the island and, being brutally honest, into his bed as well. But Liza was right; if his mother thought for a second he was fooling around with her friend's daughter she would have him married to Liza in a flash.

He dragged in a deep, calming breath. Marriage was not on his agenda, and if he ever succumbed it would only be for the production of a child to inherit the Menendez fortune. But not for years yet—he enjoyed his freedom too much, and certainly not to a girl like Liza, who he still was not sure he could trust as far as he could throw her.

His dark eyes narrowed angrily, and something darker, devious hardened in their depths. He had wanted Liza Summers from the very first moment he saw her again at the café. His thick black lashes flicked down towards the sharp line of his high cheekbones, veiling his expression, and he allowed his gaze to linger on her perfectly formed body, the slightly creased black dress she was wearing a testament to their earlier passionate encounter, and then back to her face.

Exquisite: the pale skin, the long blonde hair, the lush mouth and the brilliant blue eyes that were shooting sparks at the moment. Sparks that told him she was absolutely determined not to share his bed beneath his mother's roof.

He gritted his teeth and had to use all his famed self-control to prevent himself from sweeping her into his arms and carrying her to his bed. He had not had enough of her, not nearly enough, but he knew instinctively talking would not change her mind. He would have to be more subtle. But the irony of it was he knew they could have what was left of the night together, because his mother was spending the night with his uncle and aunt in Granada, attending their own golden-wedding dinner and a blessing in the cathedral on Sunday morning, and that they were all coming back here for lunch and the final huge party in the evening.

It was on the tip of his tongue to tell Liza, but then again he remembered she had been a very volatile teenager, and if her wildness in bed was anything to go by she hadn't changed much. She would probably blow her top and land one on him for his treachery, and any hope of resuming what they had started on the plane would be distinctly remote.

Denying the temptation to reach out to her and take up where they had left off, explore her gorgeous body once more, he shoved his hands into the pockets of his trousers, and turned his head to bark out a quick order to Manuel's retreating back.

The blue room. Liza had never heard of it, but then she had not been here for years, and she did not know if she was relieved or reluctant to part from Nick. Glancing down the long length of him, she almost changed her mind; with his hands in his pockets and the fabric of his trousers pulled taut across muscular thighs, his potent masculinity was unmistakable…

Get your head up, girl—she jerked her head back and a tide of red flooded her cheekbones. When had she become such a voyeur of men? She sighed inwardly; not men—one man. 'The blue room; I don't think I have seen it before,' she mumbled.

'Maybe not; there have been some extensive renovations since you were last here.' Nick slanted her a dark-eyed glance. 'But it is not mine, I can assure you, so I hope your honour is satisfied,' he drawled sardonically.

'Yes,' she snapped, 'thank you,' and gave him what she hoped was a cool look. He might have well as added *if you have any*, she thought as his dark eyes studied her with cynical, all masculine appraisal. And, straightening her shoulders, she stalked off after Manuel, but in one step Nick was beside her.

'In a hurry to get to bed?' he teased softly, bending his dark head to brush the words against her ear, and his husky chuckle did nothing for her attempt to remain cool.

She didn't bother to answer and a grandfather clock chimed one, disturbing the silence as Liza walked along the corridor with Nick keeping step beside her. Manuel stopped and opened a door, and, placing Liza's case inside, gave her a toothy smile and went back the way they had come.

Liza almost fell into the room, such was her haste to get away from Nick's overwhelming presence. Making love with him—no, having sex, she corrected—had done nothing to quell the heated response of her body. In fact it seemed to have sharpened every one of her senses. Now she knew what she had been missing all these years. She was so intensely aware of him she ached.

'Goodnight,' she muttered, and would have shut the door in his face, but she was too slow. Nick reached for her and pulled her into his powerful arms, his mouth came crashing down on hers, and a shocked protest was stopped in her throat as excitement spiralled inside her like a typhoon, throwing all her sense out of sight.

His hands dropped to splay against her hips and haul her into connection with the hard strength of his arousal; she felt the sudden rush of warmth between her thighs as he moved suggestively against her. She lifted her hands but Nick suddenly lifted his head, and stepped back.

'Now, that is a goodnight kiss,' he drawled mockingly,

studying her with dancing devilment in his black eyes. 'The bathroom is on the left. See you later.' And then he was gone, closing the door quietly behind him.

Liza stared at the closed door, and only after the long moment it took her to get her breathing somewhere near normal did she turn and glance around the room. A massive four-poster bed, draped in yards of the finest blue silk, and with a delicately embroidered coverlet in a deeper blue, was the central feature. Long arched windows with the same drapes hedged each side of the bed. She walked over to the bed and sat on the edge, kicking off her shoes. She glanced at the wall opposite, which housed a delicate dressing table with a fragile-looking gilt chair; her case was on the top of what looked like an antique trunk in one corner. She noted the bathroom door, again blue but edged in gold. The whole décor was blue and gold, a bit over-the-top for her taste but exquisite none the less.

With a weary sigh she stood up and, crossing to her case, she opened it and quickly unpacked her few clothes into the ornate wardrobe, and then headed for the bathroom.

The bathroom was equally as luxurious, all marble and mirrors with a large bath and shower stall. Stripping off her clothes, she took a quick shower, and, stepping out of the shower stall, she crossed to where a pile of towels were neatly stacked. She caught a glimpse of her reflection in the mirror, and stopped, blushing scarlet. The tell-tale signs of Nick's lovemaking were obvious. A slight bruise in the hollow of her throat, lower down a redness on her pale skin where the rough stubble of his chin had made a mark as he suckled her breasts. She felt her nipples tighten just at the memory.

Hastily she grabbed a large, fluffy towel from the pile and tugged it sarong-style around her slender body, refusing to look at her reflection again. The reminder was too poignant. She darted out of the bathroom, switched off the main light and dived under the sumptuous coverlet into bed by the light of a small night lamp on a table at the other side.

The traitorous thought that she could have been sharing the bed with Nick filled her mind. She lived again in her head every kiss and caress they had shared on the plane, and she wondered if she would ever experience again that passion or depth of emotion. She stirred restlessly in the bed, her body hot and wanting, she ran the tip of her tongue over her slightly swollen lips and lived again the touch of his mouth on hers. Swallowing hard, she tried to squash her wayward thoughts.

Their recent intimacy meant nothing, and she must never forget that, her common sense told her that she was only a temporary distraction for Nick Menendez. But her heart told her she was in dire danger of falling hopelessly and irretrievably in love with him. The love she had thought she felt for him as a teenager was as nothing to the power of her emotions now.

She had never known that desire could cut so deep, and she had the horrible conviction if she gave in to her feelings for him completely she would end up cut to shreds. Because the one thing she knew for certain was Nick Menendez would never see her as anything other than a brief distraction from his real life. He was a ruthlessly successful businessman of worldwide renown, and a Spanish grandee to boot, held in high esteem by all his countrymen.

She was here because his mother had invited her, albeit at Nick's instigation, of that she had no doubt. He obviously cared for his mother, and he was not averse to taking advantage of the sex Liza had quite consciously shown him was on offer. He had made it equally as plain a brief affair was all he wanted. She could hardly change her mind now. If she was honest she didn't want to…and with a bittersweet sigh she turned over and reached to extinguish the night-light.

Her heavy-lidded eyes registered another door set in the opposite wall, a dressing room maybe. She was too tired to think and, burrowing under the coverlet, in moments she was asleep.

But not peacefully, she tossed restlessly in the wide bed. In her dream she was running naked through a deep, dense forest, chasing after a huge dark, shadowy figure. Every so often the figure stopped and waited and she had a glimpse of a welcoming smile, and just when she thought she was in touching distance the figure vanished to appear well ahead of her, beckoning her on again. But the faster she ran the more naked, the more exposed she felt and the wood became thicker, darker, utterly silent, and somehow menacing.

She frowned in her sleep, fighting to escape the nightmare, her long lashes fluttering against her smooth cheek prior to opening, then inexplicably she felt a fleeting kiss as soft as a butterfly's wing across her brow. A deep, contented sigh escaped from between her softly parted lips and she closed her eyes once more in sleep, totally unaware of the man watching over her.

Drawing in a deep, steadying breath, Nick tightened the belt of his short robe, a wry smile curving his hard mouth, his dark eyes lingering on Liza's sleeping form.

He had called Carl and passed on the information that Brown was returning to Lanzarote to finalise the deal and when. But he avoided mentioning that Liza was supposed to meet up with Brown. He had lied by omission to his friend, something he had never done before. When Carl asked him about Liza he had assured him he had her under very close surveillance with him in Spain. But he was pretty sure Liza was not knowingly involved, and he would take personal responsibility for her. Carl was not happy; at the very least, he had pointed out, Liza would be a vital witness when they brought the case to court. It had taken some very persuasive argument on Nick's part to get Carl to do nothing about Liza for the moment.

Then he had paced his bedroom for over an hour, determined not to give in to the temptation of the connecting door that joined his room to hers. Even if by some miracle Liza was innocent, he knew an affair with her was bound to cause trouble, given their mothers were great friends. Never foul your own nest, he reminded himself.

But for once in his life his ardour had overcome the armour he usually had no problem keeping around his emotions. Only this witch of a woman made him weak. He dropped his dark gaze down to her firm, full breasts and involuntarily his hand moved, but firmly he shoved it in the pocket of his robe.

When he had walked through the connecting door he had fully intended joining Liza in the bed. But, seeing her lying there, her beautiful face frowning in sleep, he had bent to gently kiss away the worry from her brow, hoping she would wake. But, hearing her sigh, seeing her relax back into a deep sleep, he was content to do nothing more... Turning, he left the room.

CHAPTER SIX

LIZA shivered, feeling the chill in the air, her long eyelashes fluttering over half-open eyes. A watery sun illuminated the room in a blue haze, and she pulled the cover up to her neck and shifted sleepily. For a moment she did not know where she was, then memory returned. Of course—Spain; it was not as hot in winter here as Lanzarote.

Oh, God! Nick!

Liza twisted around and a dozen unfamiliar aches and pains in places she never knew she had made her groan. What had she done? Suddenly the erotic memories of the night before suddenly overwhelmed every other thought in her head. Had she really made love with Nick on the plane? Just the thought made her temperature rise. Nick was every woman's fantasy lover. Her whole body blushed as she recalled her own feverish abandonment to the power of his lovemaking, and she no longer felt in the least chilled.

She pushed the coverlet back down to her waist, and drew in a deep, steadying breath. So they had made love, and she was now a fully paid-up member of the mile-high club. Not something she had ever aspired to, but, being honest, she did not regret it… But it was only a holiday affair, she reminded herself quickly.

Perhaps not even that; Nick had quite happily accepted her 'No' to making love in his mother's house, and now, with the memory of the passion and the pleasure fresh in her mind, she wondered if she had been too adamant in her refusal to share his room.

She was a grown woman and perfectly entitled to explore her own sexuality, live for the moment if she wanted to, and, dear heaven, she wanted to, she thought wryly. There was no point in denying it, and, reaching her arms above her head, she stretched languorously, relishing the new sensually aware woman Nick had made her.

'Now, that is a picture worth preserving.' A deep, husky drawl shattered the silence.

Liza froze at full stretch, her gaze winging to the tall man entering the room, a tray in his hands... Nick. She studied him with helpless appreciation as he approached the bed, obviously fresh from the shower—his black hair was brushed severely back from his brow and his incredibly attractive face radiated vitality. A white towelling robe covered him from shoulder to knee, but afforded a glimpse of a hair-roughened chest. Her heart lurched at the sight of him.

'I wish I had a camera,' Nick murmured, studying her tousled appearance. With her long blonde hair tumbling around her shoulders and her arms above her head, the smooth, creamy lift of her perfect breasts was enough to make him harden. The dusky peaks tightening as he watched didn't help.

Suddenly Liza realised she had parted with the towel some time in the night, and she was naked from the waist up, and Nick's gaze was fixed on a certain part of her anatomy. Making a mad grasp for the coverlet, she pulled it up and tucked it firmly over her breasts, her face flaming.

What did you say to a man that you had had sex with on a plane? It was not a scenario she was familiar with, and her stomach cramped with nervous tension, but before she could think of a flip reply to fling back he added, 'You'd make a great centrefold.'

His words underlined her secret fear; Nick had wanted only one thing from her, and he had got it with remarkable ease. She had no one to blame but herself. She had looked at him, wanted him, and foolishly imagined she could play him at his own game, and indulge in a sophisticated love affair with no strings attached. What had been an incredible experience for her, probably ranked as an easy lay for him...

The knowledge hurt, but also stiffened her shaky resolve. If an experienced woman of the world was what Nick wanted, then that was exactly what she would be. Calling on a lifetime of ingrained good manners, she said, 'Good morning, Nick.'

Stopping at the side of the bed, Nick drew his brows together in a brief frown. He was used to a more enthusiastic welcome from the woman in his life. Why Liza was trying to appear cool when the blush in her cheeks declared otherwise, he had no idea. If he hadn't shared the most incredible sex with her, he would have said she was embarrassed. But that wasn't possible... He was not the first man she had slept with and he was not absolutely convinced she was innocent in the other matter either.

'Good morning. Is that it?' Black brows rose in sardonic amusement. 'And here I was, hoping for a kiss at least,' his dark eyes roamed with knowing sensuality over her luscious body, 'after all we have shared,' he concluded silkily and, putting the tray down on the table, he sat on the edge of the bed and reached for her hand.

Liza snatched her hand away, and fixed all her attention on the tray, unwilling to acknowledge the blatant sensuality in his look. There was a silver coffee-pot, a jug of cream, a bowl of sugar and two cups and saucers and a plate of pastries. 'You're joining me for breakfast; how nice,' she said politely, and unwillingly her gaze was drawn back to meet Nick's.

'That was the idea. I did not think you would object.' He noted her small hands clench in the coverlet and realised she was nervous. 'I thought a woman of your incredible sexual aptitude would naturally share all my appetites,' Nick teased, a slow, intimate smile curving his firm lips.

'No—yes...of course not,' Liza said in confusion, not sure if she should be flattered or furious he had found her satisfactory! Not sure he should even be here in her room, she thought, panic rising in her breast. 'What about Manuel…? Your mother…?' Liza heard her voice rising but was unable to control it as the full import of what she had allowed to happen hit her, and she turned red with embarrassment.

'Take it easy, Liza.' Nick chuckled. 'Manuel and Marta always have Sunday morning free to attend church. As for mother, she is at church in Granada, and won't be back for a while yet. She need never know that you are sharing a coffee with me.' And with a wicked grin he added, 'Stark naked beneath that sheet.'

The reminder of her nakedness made Liza blush even more, but his smile surprised her. Nick could amuse her and make her feel wanton at one and the same time. It was a lethal combination that made her even more wary. 'Oh, just shut up and pour the coffee,' she snapped.

'I do adore a woman who can take charge occasionally,' Nick drawled with a sardonic arch of one ebony brow. 'Especially in the bedroom.'

'Just pour the damn coffee,' she reiterated, her temper rising. 'I can do without sexual innuendoes first thing in the morning.'

'Pity,' Nick opined, but leant forward and filled the two cups from the jug and passed one to her. 'I guess you're not a morning person.'

Liza took hers and swallowed it down with unseemly haste, clattering the cup down on the tray with a less than steady hand. 'Well, you're wrong. I am once I have my caffeine fix.' She strove for normality, but it was difficult with Nick sitting so close. She picked up a pastry and took a bite, but she had never felt less like eating, and it was such a struggle to get the food down she didn't risk another bite, and dropped it back on the plate.

Nick chuckled, a deep, throaty sound, and reached out a long, elegant hand to sweep the tangled mass of her hair from her face. Then settled his arm around her shoulders, trapping her in the arc of his muscular chest. 'Prove it, Liza.'

His stunningly handsome face was much too close; she could see the curling length of his lashes sweep his high cheekbones, and lift to reveal eyes glinting with amusement, the firm mouth also quirking at the corners with humour.

'Prove what?' She stared up at him with a mixture of fear and anticipation.

'This.' And he covered her mouth with his own.

Her startled cry was silenced in her throat; she struggled wildly, lashing out at his great torso with curled fists. She was no man's push-over...whatever Nick Menendez thought... With a husky laugh he tipped her back against the pillows, and captured both of her flaying hands in one of his and pinned them above her head, his long body pressing her to the bed, and then he was kissing her again with a hard, deep hunger that set her on fire.

Suddenly the reason for her resistance was lost in the chaos he made of her mind. She tried to pull her hands free to hold him and with another husky chuckle Nick lifted his head and stared down into her flushed face.

'No, my lovely, I am not setting you free. I missed you in my bed last night.' Instantly she was flooded with an emotion so powerful she nearly told him, she didn't want to be free of him ever... Surely he could see that. He might be an overbearing, arrogant chauvinist, but she knew deep within her soul that he was everything she could ever want or need in a man.

She wanted back the friend she had missed, the lover she had only just discovered, and the intellectual and emotional strength that he had given so generously to a young girl before the episode that had made him her enemy.

'Your mother...' She made a weak attempt to object but her heart wasn't in it. It was in her mouth as he kissed her again. She couldn't get enough of his mouth, her tongue seeking his in a dance of desire that met and matched him with ever deeper abandon. She slid her hands over his shoulders removing his robe in the process.

His mighty chest heaved and finally Nick lifted his head, his breathing harsh and his eyes staring into hers with burning satisfaction. 'Has no one ever told you it is not a good idea to remind a man of his mother at a time like this?' he husked, the tension holding Nick's huge, powerful body taut over hers relaxing slightly as he shrugged off the robe completely. His heavy thigh slid over her slender hips and his hand splayed under her bottom, and pulled her into fierce connection with the rigid strength of his erection, sending quivering arrows of exquisite delight up from the apex of her thighs to spread through every nerve in her body.

Lifting his eyes to hers, a gleam of devilment lurking in their depths, he said throatily, 'But maybe you're right. You just reminded me of the first pleasure in a male's life—the joy of suckling.'

Leaning back, he looked his fill of the perfect mounds of her breasts, pale as magnolia with erect, rosy peaks. His hands cupped and shaped them, his thumbs teasing the straining nubs until Liza moaned her pleasure, and only then did he bury his hot mouth against her aching breasts. He laved his tongue over a rigid tip and then drew the tight bud into his mouth and suckled gently.

Helplessly Liza ran her fingers through the thick black hair of his head and urged him to deliver the same ecstasy to its aching counterpart and he obliged.

'You like that,' Nick teased and then replaced his mouth with his hands, rolling the distended, dusky nipples between his thumb and forefinger, while he trailed a burning line of kisses down over her flat stomach.

He nudged her long legs apart and, swamped in sensation after sensation, Liza helped him, and when his mouth delivered the most intimate kiss of all she welcomed it. Her slender hands grasped his wide shoulders and tremor after tremor shook her whole body, her nails dug into his flesh as the pressure heightened and heightened, until she thought she would die, and then suddenly it happened.

Nick reared up and, lifting her, plunged into the shuddering heat of her in one driving movement. '*Dios!* You feel fantastic, unbelievable.'

'So do you!' Liza cried out as she took all of him, and as he began to move she convulsed and convulsed again in a shattering climax. Her blue eyes flew wide and collided with molten black and his dark head bent and took her mouth in a deep, almost yearning kiss.

Incredibly the pleasure was rising again as Nick moved in a sensual rhythm, a driving urgency that Liza met and matched in a primitive, wild abandon that had her whimpering and crying out with pleasure. Then she felt Nick's ferocious tension, and one last desperate plunge that seemed to rock her very womb. She climaxed again as his great body shuddered over her. He groaned out something in Spanish but she was too far gone to hear, as his life force poured into her.

He had given her more pleasure than she had ever imagined existed, and yet when it was finally over, and their sweat-slicked bodies lay entwined in exhausted abandon, she felt the chill tendrils of fear snake through her tired mind.

Nick had only to appear for her to collapse into his arms. How on earth was she going to hide her helpless reaction to him? Nick was conceited and arrogant enough already about women if the gossip columns were to be believed. He did not need her adding to his tally.

'Nick, Nick.' She pushed at his broad shoulders. 'Please get up.'

'What?' His tousled head lifted and he thrust up off the pillow, releasing her from his weight. 'Flattered as I am you think I am capable,' he lay half over her and pushed her tumbled hair back from her flushed face, 'it is going to take me a little longer to recover,' he teased with a lazy smile, while his fingers toyed with her long blonde hair, smoothing a few strands down the elegant line of her neck, and over a slender shoulder.

Inflamed by his teasing comment and suddenly aware it was broad daylight, 'It's the middle of the morning,' Liza yelped. He knew damn fine what she meant, and she jerked her head free and wriggled out from under him, and dragged herself up into a sitting position. Nick collapsed down on his back and slanted her a wicked grin.

'So...' he drawled. 'You're not so innocent as to believe people only make love at night.' Nick laughed.

It was the laugh that did it. Liza glanced down at him. He looked incredible, she thought, swallowing hard, his tanned torso sleek and vibrant against the blue sheets, his black hair flopping over his brow, and his sinful black eyes glinting with mocking amusement.

'It's not in the least amusing,' she snapped, her temper rising, along with it a great dollop of embarrassment at how easily he had overcome her scruples about making love in his mother's house, conveniently ignoring that she had wanted him to!

'What will Manuel, your mother think? They might be back any minute.' She was getting into her stride. 'But then I don't suppose the great Nick Menendez ever needs to consider other people's feelings, you arrogant swine.' She was overreacting...being an absolute bitch...but with emotions raw and new tearing at her heart she didn't seem able to stop herself. Yet she knew it was her own sense of insecurity making her behave so unlike her usual calm self.

Nick jerked up, his lean face strong and taut, and for a split-second Liza saw a flash of raw fury in his dark eyes, and then his sensuous mouth curved in a faint smile.

'A stickler for propriety, Liza, and this from a girl who had no qualms about rolling around with a man in the stable of this same house,' he drawled sardonically.

All Liza's confidence and any attempt at sexual sophistication shrivelled and died. She felt as if he had knifed her in the stomach, the pain was so intense she could not look at him. Nick had never changed his mind about her. He never would, and she had foolishly thought she could have a holiday romance.

Romance! What a joke. Sex with her was just a game to him. A game he wanted to win. The same as he won everything else he set out to achieve.

Nick saw the hurt in her eyes, before she turned her head away, and he immediately wished the mocking words unsaid. He remembered his anger at finding Liza in the arms of that boy, but he had no right to throw it back at her, and especially not when he was lying naked in bed with her. How crass was that? And totally out of character for him. For once in his life he was ashamed of himself. He admired women and prided himself on his courteous treatment of any woman he became involved with.

Was he going mad? No, it was Liza; she was driving him crazy. His usual cool control deserted him as soon as he got anywhere near her. Volatile emotions were not something he had ever suffered from and it was all her fault. His dark eyes swept over her near-naked figure and he almost groaned.

Pride and anger coming to the fore, Liza made herself look at him. 'I was sixteen and foolish,' she snapped, and for a second she thought he winced. No, not the mighty Nick, she told herself. 'But I have matured and learnt better over the years.' Head high, her eyes blazing, she added, 'You obviously have not. You are still the arrogant, chauvinistic devil you always were. You still ride roughshod over any woman if it suits you.' And with that she flung her legs over the edge of the bed.

There was no way Nick was letting her get away with that; his own anger rising, he grasped her around the waist and hauled her back against him. 'Damn it, Liza.' He fell back on the bed with a squirming Liza lashing out at him. He spun her around until she was spreadeagled on top of him. 'Stop it, woman,' he growled as her hands scratched his neck and, grasping a hank of her hair, he twisted it around his wrist and pulled her head down to claim her mouth with his. He was not letting her go until her temper cooled. So he kept her where he wanted her, until he felt the fight go out of her, and only then did he let her come up for air and end the kiss.

'Call me all the names you like, Liza,' he said roughly, planting a gentle kiss on her throat, 'but you are wrong—I don't override all women.' And he kissed her again, sliding his hands down her spine and holding her close to his mighty body, his hard body… He tilted back her head, and saw the shimmer of sensual awareness she could not hide, and as he brought his hand slowly up her thigh he felt her tremble.

'In fact I rather like a woman overriding me,' he drawled throatily, and kissed her again. The next time he set her free and murmured, 'Care to try it?' Her hands were on his shoulders and his were around her thighs as he lowered her onto him.

Liza gasped out loud, her head thrown back, as he filled her so completely she thought she would faint with the pleasure. She moved with unconscious sensuality. She had never felt anything like it. Nick's hands slid up her spine and urged her forward and he captured the peak of one perfectly shaped breast in his mouth, and her anger, her resentment no longer existed. Only the man sheathed deep inside her.

A long time later Nick chuckled, a deep, throaty sound. 'I hate to tell you, sweetheart, but it is almost noon.' He heard her choked gasp, and, dropping a light kiss on her swollen lips, he swung his legs off the bed and pulled on his robe.

'Oh, my God!' Mouth open in shock, Liza could do nothing when Nick bent down and caught her to him, and claimed a long kiss. Instinctively she splayed her palms on his broad chest, drowning in the incredible sweetness of the sensual but surprisingly tender kiss.

When he released her Nick saw the heated longing in

her eyes. He knew perfectly well how he affected her. But he straightened up before he gave in to the temptation to join her in the bed again.

'Don't worry, there is no hurry, Liza. Lunch is about one and I'll meet you downstairs.' He noted the high colour in her lovely face. 'And don't be embarrassed. You are a very welcome guest in this house, a family friend, and I promise you will enjoy your stay.'

The kiss, the endearment and his attempt at reassurance warmed Liza's heart, and, as she relaxed slightly, her full lips curved in a smile. 'You'd better or I might request a refund.'

His stunning dark eyes glinted devilishly down at her. 'A refund—no... A replay—yes.' And he headed for the door, leaving her to interpret that as she wished.

Half an hour later Liza stood and surveyed her reflection in the cheval glass. She had swept her hair back, and knotted a white silk scarf around it. A touch of lipstick and a moisturiser for her skin was all the make-up she needed. She had opted to wear a crisp white shirt and navy trousers, a matching leather belt accentuated her narrow waist and on her feet she wore soft hide pumps. Yes, she would do... She was a bit early but she could not wait to see Nick again. She wanted to pinch herself to make sure she was not dreaming. Niculoso Menendez was her lover and she felt like shouting it to the heavens.

Instead she made her way along the hall towards the kitchen. Anna Menendez had usually kept lunch a pretty flexible affair, and she doubted anything would have changed. Five minutes later Manuel was showing her into the dining room, and she saw to her surprise there were several other guests there.

She hesitated just inside the door, suddenly overcome by nerves. She couldn't see Nick anywhere. She scanned the room again and almost turned and ran when she realised he wasn't there, and the other guests were all expensively attired, the men in suits and the women in designer clothes.

When she was a child visiting in the height of summer, lunch had been a casual affair and always eaten alfresco. Her own common sense should have told her in the middle of winter the dining room was a more likely venue. Except she had no common sense around Nick, and in her haste to meet up with him again she hadn't thought. But Nick could have warned her. With all these people he must have known lunch was going to be a formal affair.

She saw Señora Menendez, and when she had recovered her poise sufficiently Liza made her way towards her. After all, she was here at the lady's invitation. A family friend, as Nick had said. No one knew they were lovers, and if she found the thought vaguely disturbing she hid it from the woman she was approaching.

Liza had always liked Nick's mother, a small, dark, very pretty woman, rather like Audrey Hepburn she had always thought. Today Anna Menendez was wearing what was obviously a Chanel suit. The other guests consisted of two elderly couples whom Liza had never seen before, and two young couples.

She felt rather underdressed and she could kill Nick for not telling her what to expect, and leaving her alone to face strangers. But with instant death to Nick, her nemesis, not an option…Liza straightened her shoulders and with all the poise she could muster she said, 'Hello, Anna.'

'Liza, how wonderful to see you again, it has been far too long.' And suddenly Liza was being kissed on both cheeks and enveloped in a cloud of very expensive French perfume. For the next ten minutes she was subjected to a flurry of questions about her own mother and her work, and finally another invitation.

'Your mother is coming at the end of March for Easter. We have not seen each other since she married again, but apparently Jeff has agreed to look after the business, so I am really looking forward to her stay,' Anna told her. 'You must come with her, we can have a real girlie break, shopping and gossiping. You must not be a stranger again. I was really angry with Niculoso for taking off to Lanzarote yesterday when he had promised faithfully to be in Granada for his Uncle Thomas's celebration. But I totally forgive him because he found you.' And, lifting a small, elegant hand, she patted Liza's cheek.

'It is great to be here. And I am sorry to hear you have been unwell,' and, studying the older woman's face, Liza was struck by the fact Anna looked positively blooming, her dark eyes, so like her son's, were clear and twinkling merrily.

Anna gave her a most peculiar look. 'Did Nick tell you that?'

'Well, not exactly,' Liza had to amend honestly when she thought about what Nick had actually said last night. But he had known perfectly well Liza had jumped to the conclusion his mother was ill, and played on her sympathetic nature. 'He said you had been a bit down, but you look great.'

'Oh, he probably meant the small chest infection I had a couple of weeks ago, but I am fine now, never better. But you know what men are, always exaggerating. Yesterday he left me a note saying he had to attend an emergency meeting with Carl Dalk and took off in the jet to Lanzarote. I doubt if it was really that vital and I expected Nick to bring Carl back with him. But instead he brought you, dear, for which I am very grateful. You didn't happen to meet Carl, did you?'

Liza shook her head. 'No.' Her smooth brow creased in a puzzled frown at Anna's revelation.

'Maybe that's just as well. He is very handsome and very wealthy, but what those two get up to together is anybody's guess. I know Carl still encourages Nick in the extreme sports, long after the pair of them should have given up such things.' She shook her dark head. 'Still, it is lovely to have you here, and you will come back with your mother?'

Liza smiled down at Anna, feeling slightly better. 'It is great to be here,' she responded. 'As for March, I will try.'

But as she said it she knew she would not. Her affair, if
that was what it was, with Nick was for a limited period,
and she would probably never see Anna again after this.

In fact, the more she thought about it away from Nick's
disturbing presence, the more her suspicions were aroused.
She was beginning to wonder why Nick had been so eager
for her to come to Spain with him for the party. Was it just
her sex appeal, as he said? Hardly likely, she thought ruefully, because she'd never thought she had much. Plus
Nick's story to his mother about an urgent meeting in
Lanzarote with this Carl chap didn't ring true. Nick had
spent almost the whole day and the evening with her. He
could hardly have meant the two-minute visit to the building site…could he…?

'Is Carl Dalk in the construction industry?' Liza asked
Anna.

'No.' Anna grinned, and stretched out an arm to show
Liza a brilliant diamond bracelet. 'This is Carl's business,
diamonds, but I get the impression from Nick all is not—'

Nick walked up behind Liza just in time to hear Carl's
name mentioned.

'Ah, Mamma. You have met Liza,' he interrupted
quickly, cutting out whatever his mother was going to say.
'Now, I want to steal her away from you for a moment to
introduce her to Uncle Thomas.'

Liza tensed as his large hand curved around her upper
arm in a firm grip. Nice of him to arrive at last, but what
had got into him, interrupting the conversation like that?
She shot him a puzzled sidelong glance, her resentment
rising when she realised he was dressed in a perfectly tailored silver-grey suit, white shirt and silk tie. He looked
magnificent and his assured masculinity took her breath
away, but when her gaze reached his darkly handsome face
she saw he was smiling but the humour didn't reach his
eyes; instead his dark gaze was veiled, masking all expression.

Anna Menendez, at the age of sixty, was nobody's fool.

'You do that.' Her small head swivelled between the tall, beautiful girl and her huge son. The tension between the two was palpable and she knew her only son too well not to realise he was up to something. If it was what she thought it was she could not be more pleased, but at thirty-five Niculoso was very set in his ways. He had the same charm and charisma as her late husband—more, in fact. But he also had an arrogant, cynical edge where women were concerned that his father, as a happily married man, had never suffered from. 'But I will speak to you later, Niculoso.'

Two pairs of identical dark eyes clashed, and Nick was the first to look away.

Seeing the look between mother and son, Liza knew something was going on here she did not understand. 'Wait a minute,' she began, turning a frowning gaze on Nick. 'I—'

'Later,' Nick said smoothly, tightening his grip on Liza's arm. 'My uncle is dying to meet you.' And he propelled her across the room in front of him. She looked stunning, and her behind in those trousers was doing wicked things to his libido.

Nick could not believe it! He had never known a woman in his life take so little time to get dressed, and he had known plenty. It was barely an hour ago when he had left Liza in bed, for heaven's sake! It never entered his head she would get to his mother before he did. Heaven knew what his mother had said. But he had a damn good idea he was going to find out, and not just from Liza, but from his mother as well. Not something he was looking forward to. He doubted the man was ever born who could hide anything successfully from his own mother.

Standing at Nick's side, Liza silently fumed, *His uncle was dying to meet her?* Since when? she wondered acidly. She didn't believe it for a minute. Then, running over the conversation with Anna, she suddenly stiffened, shooting Nick an angry glance. 'You…' She tried to pull her arm free. He had not wanted her talking to his mother, that much was obvious.

'I said later,' Nick growled between gritted teeth, and then in a complete turn-about, charm oozing from every pore, 'Uncle Thomas,' he addressed the small man in front of them, 'I want you to meet Liza; she is the daughter of Pamela Summers, Mamma's English friend.'

In a flurry of introductions Liza met Thomas's wife, Ellen, her brother, Paulo, and his wife, and discovered the two young couples were not couples at all, but the sons and daughters of Thomas and Paulo; she caught the name Marco...he looked vaguely familiar, but the rest of the names were lost.

In the general conversation that followed Liza realised Thomas and Ellen were celebrating their golden wedding. Last night there'd been a dinner at their home in Granada. The dinner Nick had missed... Today a family lunch with Anna and tonight Anna was hosting a party for all their friends and relatives.

'I want to talk to you,' Liza muttered in a swift aside to Nick as with a hand at her back he led her to her seat at the exquisitely prepared dining table. 'This is a family lunch and I feel terrible, an interloper...'

But the hand Nick had at her spine slipped around her slender waist, and halted them both. He stared down at her with intent black eyes. 'You are not an interloper. I told you before, you're a welcome guest.'

'So you say,' she muttered, 'but you could have told me...I'm not dressed.'

Nick shrugged a wide shoulder. 'You look pretty well-covered to me,' he drawled sardonically.

'That is not the point,' she snapped crossly, but before she could get another word out Nick had pulled out a chair and, with his hand on her shoulder, urged her down onto it.

His dark head bent towards hers, and he said with sibilant

softness, 'Behave yourself, Liza…nothing must spoil Thomas's day.'

Trust him to think only of the man in the celebration and not Ellen, the wife, the chauvinistic pig… 'What about…?' His long fingers dug into her shoulder in a none-too-subtle threat.

'Not now, Liza.' His look flashed her a warning that she could not fail to recognise. 'Later,' he commanded and sat down on the chair next to her, his hand slipping from her shoulder to land on her thigh beneath the cover of the table-cloth.

Liza tensed in shock at his boldness and her own instant reaction to the long finger that caressed her inner thigh. She knocked his hand away, and glanced warily around, and only then did Liza realise the rest of the company had fallen silent and were watching her and Nick with varying degrees of interest. She wanted to slide under the table with embarrassment.

Surprisingly the lunch was not as bad as Liza had feared; the food was superb, and she might have quite enjoyed the spirited and lively conversation that ensued, except she could not dismiss from her mind the growing suspicion that somehow Nick's reason for bringing her to Spain was not just because of his mother and the instant attraction between them, as she had believed.

Even admitting it had been pure coincidence that Anna had called while Liza was with Nick last night, Nick had deliberately mentioned her presence, knowing his mother would do what she had done and invite her to stay.

Liza had the nasty feeling she was somehow Nick's second choice. His mother had thought he was meeting a Carl Dalk and bringing him back to the party. But Liza couldn't see when Nick had had the time to meet this Dalk chap. Nick had told her he had just come from the airport and then he had spent virtually the whole day with her. Surely in the normal course of conversation he would have mentioned an urgent meeting; instead they had visited a building site for a few minutes. Maybe the two men had had some dangerous, illegal stunt in mind, like bunjee jumping into a volcanic crater in the Timanfaya National Park. According to Anna they were partners in such escapades, and then perhaps Carl Dalk had not turned up.

'More wine, Liza?'

Liza looked up with a start, her blue eyes searching his handsome face; his expression was bland, his dark eyes revealing nothing. 'No, thank you,' she said firmly, recognising Nick was very good at hiding his feelings. But how much more was he hiding…?

He had been very insistent she come to the party. He had not actually lied and said his mother was ill, but he knew she had thought that was what he meant. She needed to talk to him, and she needed some answers; something smelt fishy, and it wasn't the steak on her plate. But before she could pursue the subject Uncle Thomas asked her why a lovely girl like her was not married. Which caused great gales of laughter and a sardonic glance from Nick.

'Because I have never found a man that suits me,' she said with a grin. 'Until I met you, Thomas, but unfortunately you're taken,' and banished her suspicions to the back of her mind in the laughter that followed.

The wine flowed freely, and when the older couples started reminiscing about the distant past, long before the rest were born, Anna suggested Nick take Liza and his cousins outside and show them his latest addition to the stables, a particularly fine racehorse.

Nick was standing, his hand on the halter of the magnificent black stallion, and smiling with obvious pride of ownership as he stroked the sleek, glossy neck. Everyone enthused over the animal.

Man and beast looked magnificent, Liza acknowledged. Two of a kind, superb male specimens. Nick looked so breathtakingly good-looking, devastatingly cool and in control of the animal. Choking back the sudden swell of emotion just watching him caused, she tore her gaze away, suddenly afraid he had been controlling her with the same accomplished ease.

She glanced around and a split-second later the colour drained from her face and involuntarily she shivered as she realised exactly where she was. The horse was in the one stall she had never wanted to see again.

Liza lifted appalled eyes just as Nick glanced in her direction, and the brilliant smile on his lean, strong face vanished as their eyes met, his expression suddenly harsh, and all her suspicions resurfaced with a vengeance.

Spinning around, Liza dashed back out of the stable, and for a moment leant against the wall, taking deep, steadying breaths, hating herself for panicking in front of everyone. It seemed in Nick's company she could not help but regress into the besotted child she had once been, and it had to stop. Straightening up, she set off across the cobbled courtyard towards the house. To hell with Nick and his horses, she had had enough of both for the moment.

Nick handed the halter to Marco. 'You four have a look around. I need to check on something,' he said before he followed Liza out.

Liza had only gone a dozen yards when a strong arm wrapped around her waist and hauled her hard against a taut male body.

'Where do you think you're going?' Nick demanded roughly.

'Anywhere away from you,' she shot back defiantly. She had made an enormous mistake. Nick did not need to say anything; it had been there in his face as he had glanced at her. He still thought she was no better than the slut he had accused her of being years ago, and she had compounded the notion by freely coming to Spain with him and succumbing with wild abandonment to his lovemaking. Whatever his reason for wanting her here, she was pretty sure it was not just his stated desire to sleep with her. He could have any woman he wanted, after all.

Nick hauled her around in one powerful arm and marched her towards the back of the house without a word.

'Let go of me, you great brute,' Liza cried, trying to break free.

'No.' His dark eyes without a glimmer of expression rested for a moment on her flushed, defiant face. 'It was insensitive of me, I know, but save the recriminations until we get back to the house,' he advised hardly.

'Why the hell should I?' Liza was hurting and suspicious and furious with herself for being such a push-over.

A black brow lifted sardonically. 'Because this is a celebration, remember, fifty years married, and you are not going to cause a scene. Though how any man could stand a woman for fifty years is beyond me,' he bit out cynically.

Hectic colour tinged her face. 'Me, cause a scene. Your poor mother—'

'Enough,' Nick exploded. He was not used to having his actions questioned by anyone, and certainly not by a slip of a girl. Acting on impulse, he swung her off her feet and carried her through the kitchen, oblivious to the astonished looks of Manuel and the staff, and didn't stop until he reached her room, and flung her on the bed.

'Right, Liza, let's have it,' he demanded roughly.

For a stunned moment Liza thought he was referring to sex. Her face paled, and then a swift tide of red suffused her cheeks. 'Why, you—'

'My, but you do have a one-track mind...' Nick drawled mockingly, the knowing light in his deep brown eyes telling her he had read her mind.

'Hardly surprising around the Spanish Stud,' she flung back.

'Ah, Liza,' he glanced down at her, viewing her angry expression with an indulgent smile, 'you should not believe everything you read in the gossip columns.' He grinned smugly. 'Though I didn't hear you complaining this morning—quite the contrary.'

His impregnable confidence in his masculine prowess

made her temper rise to boiling point, and, leaping off the bed, she marched up to him.

'I am glad you think it is funny.' She poked him in the chest with a finger. 'You conniving bas—' Her wrist was caught in an iron grip and the insults stuck in her throat.

'No one talks to me like that.' Nick's hard jawline clenched and glittering black eyes scanned her angry face. 'Especially not a woman of your kind,' he told her icily.

'My kind?' Liza repeated, a terrible coldness taking the place of her anger that he could be so callous.

'You know what I mean, Liza. I was not your first lover and I certainly won't be your last, though if your overreaction is anything to go by your past lovers must have been pretty ineffectual. You were as up for it as I was from the moment we met again. Why the outrage now?' he demanded with a cruelty she would not have thought him capable of. 'Simply because you found yourself in a stable that held a memory of a past indiscretion?'

Colour tinged her cheeks; she did not need to be reminded of her helpless surrender to his sexual expertise, and certainly not of her juvenile reaction to him years ago. 'That is a filthy thing to say…but about what I would expect from a man of your morals.' And, blue eyes flashing flames, she stared furiously up into Nick's face. 'But this isn't about sex,' she said, fighting to retain her temper. 'There is something going on here that I don't understand. Who the hell is Carl Dalk? Your mother thought you had an urgent meeting with him yesterday, and I can't believe you would lie to your own mother but you told me you had just come from the airport when we met, and you spent the whole day with me. I am not conceited enough to think a man like you would dump an emergency meeting for me.' Once Liza started listing her suspicions she could not stop. 'Your mother thought this Carl chap was coming back with you.' She fixed angry, assessing eyes on his hard face. 'And another thing, last night you let me think your mum was ill, and yet when I met your mum she said she has never felt better in her life. Don't take me for a fool, Nick.'

Nick absorbed her flushed and angry face with arrogant detachment. He had known it was coming but he had hoped to divert her. Liza's mention of Carl was a little too close for comfort. Narrowed dark eyes met brilliant blue and he was impressed—not many people stood up to him or even tried. He supposed he should be flattered that at least Liza did not want to think him capable of lying to his own mother, but what to tell her?

'Watch it, Liza, your paranoia is showing,' he tried to tease, but she met his attempt at humour with an elegantly elevated brow. She was an intelligent woman and wanted answers, Nick recognised, and humour wasn't going to do it for her.

'Just answer the question,' Liza demanded.

'Carl Dalk is an old friend of mine and, contrary to what you assumed, I did speak with him yesterday afternoon, after I left you at your hotel.'

'Oh.' Liza supposed that was possible, but it didn't strike her as very urgent if he could wait all day to meet the man. 'Not that much of an emergency, then,' she prompted defensively, beginning to wonder if maybe he was right and she was being paranoid...

'My, my, Liza, you do have a suspicious mind in that very lovely body. As for Mamma, I told you she was feeling down.' He shrugged a shoulder. 'You drew your own conclusion.'

'And you let me!' Liza exclaimed, amazed at the sheer gall of the man. 'You dragged me a thousand miles to sle...to Spain...' She stuttered to a stop, having almost said *to sleep with me* and stared at him, scanning his strong dark features, the devastating face, looking for some guilt... She found none. Instead to her shame her anger faded beneath the mesmerising effect of his powerful presence. She shook her head; she didn't understand. 'Why?'

'First, I don't recall any force involved. You accepted

my mother's invitation, before I told you she had been ill. I just helped reinforce your decision when, like a typical woman, you looked like changing your mind,' Nick contradicted silkily as two strong hands curved around her shoulders. 'As to the why—because I wanted you; it is that simple.' His dark head lowered, his lips feathering across hers, and she trembled as the pressure of his kiss deepened, the hard heat of his mouth burning on her own.

'No,' Liza groaned in denial, but couldn't prevent the familiar heat igniting in her traitorous body.

Nick stifled a groan of pent-up desire and ended the kiss. He could not tell her the whole truth, not if he wanted to keep her safe and in his bed, and suddenly he discovered keeping her in his bed was becoming of vital importance to him. The enormity of the thought shocked him.

Defence mechanisms clicking in, Nick stilled then eased away slightly. 'OK.' Her head was thrown back, her eyes were closed and her cheeks were hot with colour. He couldn't resist so he nuzzled the elegant line of her throat, heard her soft moan and sensed her fluctuating inclinations as expertly as he read the stock market.

When he finally lifted his head he saw her eyes open and the flicker of disappointment in their depths she was unable to hide. His smile was a battle between contrition and triumph. He was still in control. 'Be honest, Liza, you know the sexual chemistry between us is too powerful to ignore,' he prompted with total conviction.

The chemistry she could not deny, and did not try to. 'But why did you want me to speak to your mother in the first place?' she asked shakily, feeling her way through a minefield of conflicting emotions. He implied it was because he wanted her... She should be flattered...but something still niggled. He was an experienced man, and her own innate honesty forced her to admit she would have gone to bed with him anywhere, and he had to know that. 'We could have stayed in Lanzarote,' with no family and friends to bother them, she thought, but didn't say it.

Nick slipped a hand around the nape of her neck; as she felt his fingers lacing through her hair and trying to ignore the racing of her pulse and the heat curling through her at his closeness, she repeated, 'Why?'

'Simple expedience, Liza.' His dark gaze held hers with a narrow-eyed intensity that tore at her fragile control. 'I had to return to Spain, because my mother and I are the hosts of this party tonight.'

'Oh, yes,' Liza murmured. She had forgotten that and felt a fool.

'Yes, Liza.' And he tilted her head towards his. 'And, having just found you, I could not bear to let you go.'

Fantastic as it sounded, Liza wanted to believe him, she wanted Nick to feel just a fraction of what she felt for him, and she told herself his explanation was reasonable. But, held close to his hard body with one arm around her waist and with his other hand in her hair, she had a suspicion he could have told her black was white and she would have believed him. The raw sexuality he exuded was an almost tangible force that enveloped her practically to the exclusion of everything else. But not quite...

'You could have just asked me.' Liza stated the obvious, while unable to restrain a thrill of pleasure that a man like Nick might actually want her so desperately.

'And you would have agreed to take off to another country with me for a party. Just like that?' Nick stated with a sardonic lift of one black brow. 'Don't forget I remember you of old, Liza, and did not fancy getting my face slapped for my cheek.'

'No, probably not,' she conceded.

'So I am forgiven, and that is our first fight over and forgotten and we can get back to more satisfying pursuits,' he declared huskily.

No asking forgiveness, just declaring it—how like Nick, she thought dazedly as he asserted his masculine power in a wordless possessive look that ripped through the last of her defences. 'You're impossible,' Liza said, her lips parting in a wry smile. 'Your arrogant conceit never ceases to amaze me.' But the soft glow in her expression took the sting from her words.

His dark head bent and his hand in her hair tightened, tilting her face up to his, and he brought his mouth gently down on hers. 'Ah, but admit it, Liza. You would not have me any other way.' He mouthed the words against her lips and then stopped her outraged gasp by the seductive invasion of his tongue.

Later she might regret it, but with pulses pounding, and the familiar ache of desire coursing through her body, her hands stroked up and over his broad shoulders, and quite simply clung...

Nick's mouth lifted from hers, his deep brown eyes darkening with passion. 'I would continue,' he murmured throatily, 'but I think I have embarrassed you enough for one day carrying you up here,' he said ruefully, studying her beautiful, flushed face. 'Being late for Mamma's party would really feed the gossip mill.'

'You're right.' Liza sighed her agreement.

'I always am,' Nick stated outrageously, and he kissed her again. The passion of his kiss was so overwhelming that she could not immediately pull herself together when he raised his head and stepped back. 'And, before you ask, the party is formal, and I will be back here to escort you at seven.'

'I'll have to find something to wear,' she blurted, grateful for something normal to focus on when Nick made pea soup of her usually astute deductive powers.

'You do that.' And, swooping down, he brushed her mouth with his again. 'But I much prefer you naked.' And left.

CHAPTER SEVEN

STANDING under the soothing spray of the shower, Liza tried to make some sense of the past two days. She had woken up in her hotel yesterday morning expecting to attend a seminar for the next two weeks with her boss. Now she was in Spain, having spent a crazy, fantasy few hours of passion with Nick Menendez, and if she was not very careful she was in danger of falling in love with him all over again.

The thought stopped her cold. No, she could not love him...must not, but she had a sinking feeling it might already be too late. What on earth had possessed her to believe she could have a holiday romance and walk away unscathed from a man like Nick? She supposed it was a compliment that he wanted her so badly and, knowing he had to return to Spain, he had got his mother to invite her. But how long would he desire her, and could she survive the ending of what was only a lustful affair to Nick?

Usually she was the sanest, most conservative of women. So what had happened to her? Nick had happened to her...

Turning off the shower, she stepped out and, wrapping a bath sheet around her body, she padded into the bedroom. Ten minutes later, dried and wearing only white lace briefs, she sat in front of the dressing-table mirror drying her hair, a dreamy smile playing around her lips as she reran in her mind the fantastic coincidence of meeting Nick again. She remembered every moment, every touch, every word...

When suddenly she realised just what had been nagging at the back of her mind since last night. When she had met Nick yesterday morning he had taken a great deal of interest in her job. She had told him she worked for Stubbs and

100

Company and she was in Lanzarote with her boss for a conference and all about her unexpected break. But she was sure she'd never mentioned Henry Brown by name.

Yet last night over dinner when Nick had been teasing her about being a lap dancer and suggested she might have a high-powered lover, she had responded that that was classified information.

But then Nick had said he had heard her boss *Henry Brown* was nowhere near as discerning about his love life and he knew Brown was married.

Thinking about it now, she recalled a brief moment when something had struck her as odd, but she had been so busy trying to act the sophisticate and hold up her side of the conversation she had banished it to the back of her mind. But the more she thought about it, she was absolutely certain she had not mentioned Brown by name earlier in the day. Plus, *how* had Nick known she was sharing a suite with her boss? For a man who ran a huge international corporation it was odd Nick seemed to know an awful lot about a small company like Stubbs and Company, and had even asked more. As her imagination took flight, industrial espionage sprang to mind...

Later still, wearing the dress she had packed originally to wear at the gala to end the seminar, she studied her finished image in the long mirror. With her long hair swept back into a French pleat, ending in a loose tumble of hair on the top of her head, and the careful application of eyeshadow and mascara and her lips outlined in a dusky-rose lip gloss, she looked cool and poised. But she was nowhere near as cool inside; she could not banish her suspicion of Nick's motive from her mind.

Sighing, she turned away from the mirror, and slipped her feet into three-inch-heeled silver sandals that matched the silver strapless dress she was wearing. Maybe Nick was right and she was paranoid? She straightened up, and adjusted the chain of the diamond crucifix at her throat. She looked good, she was attractive, so why was she plagued with insecurities? Maybe that was what love did to one?

No, she was not in love, Liza told herself; she needed to get a grip. So far she had allowed Nick to call all the shots and it had to stop. She wanted some straight answers to some straight questions from the man. If they were not forthcoming then she was going to leave tomorrow. If Nick was telling the truth and he really had a great desire for her, he would follow her, and if he didn't then better to know now before she got in too deep.

The door flung open, and Nick walked into the room. '*Dios,* Liza.' He stopped, his dark eyes roaming over her from the cool beauty of her face and lower to where the silver strapless gown revealed the gentle swell of her breasts, then lovingly clung to every perfect inch of her to end mid-thigh. She had legs to die for… 'You look incredible.' She reminded him of some fabled Valkyrie, a Norse goddess, and he felt the most inexplicable pain in his chest.

'Have you ever heard of knocking?' Liza smiled but stepped back as he walked towards her, an unmistakable gleam in his eyes.

'We are way past that stage.' Nick's glance slanted meaningfully at the bed, and back to roam slowly over her once again.

'You maybe, but not me,' Liza said firmly. But her pulse was racing at the sight of him. In a formal dinner suit he was devastating.

'Am I missing something here?' Nick asked drily, and caught her hand, bringing it up towards his chest. 'I thought we were past playing games, but if you insist on formality…' He bowed his dark head and kissed her hand.

Her fingers curled against the tingling sensations shooting up her arm, and when he lifted his head she saw the desire tinged with anger in the depths of his dark eyes.

'Not formality,' she countered steadily, 'but good manners never come amiss. And I told you last night I am not sleeping with you when your mother is at home, and this

time I mean it.' Her blue eyes clashed with his. He was
watching her intently, a curious expression on his starkly
handsome face.

What on earth was she doing lecturing Nick Menendez
on manners? She grimaced at the thought. 'I'll forgive you
this time, Nick.' She opted to tease. 'Now, where is the
party?'

'I know where I would like it to be,' he drawled mockingly with another glance at the bed, 'but it seems that is
not an option.' And tightening his hold on her hand, he
added, 'anyway, duty calls. But, be warned, we are leaving
at midnight for a drive if that is the only way to get you
alone.' And to illustrate his point he bent his arrogant dark
head, and ran his tongue along the curve of her breasts
above the bodice of the dress.

Instant excitement lanced through her body. 'What do
you think you're doing?' she jerked back.

'Please, Liza, no innocent outrage, we both know it is a
lie,' Nick drawled cynically, staring down into her brilliant
blue eyes. She was stunningly beautiful, and incredibly
sexy, but he was a lot older and a lot smarter than he was
when he had hungered after her in a stable all those years
ago. Life had taught him that women were devious crea-
tures, and this one was probably more treacherous than
most. Two hours ago he had left Liza eager and wanting,
but something had changed, and why the hell he was trying
to protect her he did not know.

'Come on,' he said flatly, 'we'll be late,' and with her
hand still in his he pulled her out of the bedroom.

Nick had just spent a painful half-hour being lectured by
his own mother on his relationships with women; he did
not need any more hassle from the fairer sex, though he
was beginning to think there was nothing fair about them.

His mother had told him quite frankly she knew perfectly
well he used women for his own gratification with no
thought of commitment. But if he had any idea of treating
the lovely Liza in the same way he could forget it.

If any other person talked to him as his mother had done he would have felled them. But she was his mother so he had contained his temper, though it had been a near thing when she had caustically informed him that she was certain the reason Liza had stayed away since she was sixteen had to be because Nick had made a pass at the girl and terrified her, and he was not to repeat the mistake. Liza was a *good girl.*

He'd almost lost it then and told his mother the truth. Good in bed, yes! But as for the rest... The injustice of it still made him see red.

Tightening his grip on Liza's arm, he hurried her through the long corridors to the main part of the house. Dark eyes hard, he glanced at her exquisite profile; he was trying to save the woman from almost certain arrest, but to hear his mother talking he was one stop short of a sex maniac.

But, even worse for a man who prided himself on being in control, he knew he was on very shaky ground. Plus, if he took Liza at her word, his sex life was down the drain as long as they stayed here.

What a dilemma. He was between a rock and a hard place and he did not like it. Damn it to hell! He was much too wily and jaded a male to fall for typical feminine ploys, and rescuing damsels in distress had gone out in the last century with the advance of feminism. So what had possessed him to act like a misguided knight to save Liza? He had no answer, or not one he was prepared to admit to. But he had discovered it was not easy trying to act the white knight, especially when he was thinking below his waist most of the time, and that was Liza's fault as well.

Liza was quietly fuming. 'Wait a minute, Nick.' He had almost dragged her through the house without giving her time to catch her breath, but now they could hear the music playing and they had almost reached the entrance to the huge salon.

'Before we go any further,' Liza stopped and that got his attention, his dark eyes glancing impatiently down at her,

'I want to know how you knew the name of my boss Henry Brown. I never told you but you mentioned him first at dinner last night, and also how did you know I was sharing a suite with him?'

So she had finally noticed the one real slip he'd made. He wasn't surprised; she was an intelligent girl. 'You have a very low opinion of your own attraction if you have to keep searching for a reason to be with me, other than sex,' he said bluntly. 'And a very fertile imagination, Liza; a bit of business espionage, something like that on your mind, hmm?' And tightening his grip on her wrist, he added, 'I don't usually explain my actions to a woman, but I will make an exception in your case. It is quite simple; when I arrived at your hotel last night I asked for you at Reception. The girl there was very chatty,' Nick opined hardly. 'She told me you were sharing a suite with a Henry Brown.'

His crack about a low opinion of herself and sex hit a nerve, but it did not stop her questioning his response. Was a receptionist supposed to give out that kind of information? Liza didn't think so. But then, remembering her first sight of Nick in the hotel, leaning on the desk laughing with the girl, and her own jealous reaction, she had to accept his answer was perfectly feasible. Nick could charm anything out of any woman, she thought drily, and felt stupid for asking. 'Do you mind? You're hurting me,' she snapped.

'Not at all.' He dropped her wrist as if it was something unpleasant. 'It would never do for us to be seen holding hands, family friend and all that,' he mocked.

'Señor.' Manuel appeared at Nick's side, and said something softly in Spanish.

Nick placed a hand at the base of Liza's spine. 'Go on in—I have to take a call.' And he was gone before she could protest, disappearing into what she knew was the study. Liza stood for a moment, her eyes on the closed door. Industrial espionage was a bit wild, but she was still not convinced that Nick didn't have some agenda of his own, and it wasn't just a helpless fascination for her body, she was sure.

A crowd of people entered the hall and reluctantly she gave up trying to fathom Nick and walked into the large salon. The party had already started and there had to be over a hundred people there.

A small dance floor had been laid at one end and a trio was playing lively Latino music. Liza glanced around but she hardly knew anyone.

Seeing a passing waiter balancing a tray, she gratefully accepted a glass of champagne and took a good swallow, cursing Nick under her breath for deserting her, but at the same time realising it was inevitable. He had passed her off as a friend of the family, and that was how she must stay. Deviousness was not in her nature, but Nick was a master at it. He had dismissed her honest question as not important and sadly she realised it was not important to him, because *she* was not important to him. He didn't actually care how she felt as long as he got what he wanted.

Liza could not tolerate deceit of any kind, and unfortunately, Liza realised, drawing on the harsh lesson she had learned nine years ago, wanting someone was not enough. Respect and trust had to be part of the equation, not to mention love. Better to nip the affair in the bud now, before Nick actually broke her heart. Her decision was made; she was definitely going to leave in the morning.

She only had to get through tonight. Draining her glass, she placed it on a convenient table and, straightening her shoulders, she lifted her head and looked around.

Nick leaned against his desk in the study and listened in mounting anger as Carl filled him in on the latest developments.

The case had taken a nasty twist. Two men had beaten up Daidolas's receptionist at the shop—probably the sailors the police were trying to find. They knew there had been a delivery and they wanted to know where Daidolas was;

he owed them money or they would take diamonds. The terrified receptionist had revealed an English girl had delivered a parcel but she knew nothing about it, or where her boss was. The police had checked Liza's hotel, and worse was to follow: somebody had called and asked to speak to Mr Brown's PA, and the talkative girl on the desk, probably the same one Nick had spoken to the night before, had quite happily revealed Liza had left with a Señor Menendez, and that Liza's luggage had been sent for a few hours later.

Nick cursed the downside of being a high-profile businessman as Carl informed him it was more than likely the two men knew Liza was in Spain with him and everyone had heard of the Menendez stud.

A few telephone calls later and Nick left his study, his handsome face hard and slightly grey beneath his tan. He had arranged for round-the-clock security on the estate, by his own men and the local police. But he was still not content. It was a big party, and with over a hundred guests anybody could have slipped onto the property in the bustle of arrivals. He wanted Liza out of here.

Liza placed her empty glass on a window ledge, and looked around the crowd of people. There was still no sign of Nick. Fortunately at that moment Thomas's son, Marco, appeared at her side.

'The lovely Liza, and alone. Can I have this dance?' he asked with a grin.

She was relieved to see a friendly face, having been introduced to him at lunch. Marco was a young man in his twenties, very attractive and very aware of it; she had an inkling he was a bit of a flirt, but it was just what she needed.

'Yes, thank you, Marco.' And when he put his hand around her waist and led her through the crowd to the dance floor, she felt none of the tension Nick's touch aroused in her.

'You don't remember me, do you?'

'Should I?' Liza grinned; he was a handsome young man.

'I stayed here once when you were here. I was twelve and you were sixteen and I had the most enormous crush on you, but you only had eyes for one of the grooms.'

'Oh, no.' And she laughed it off with, 'Was I that obvious?'

'Only to me, probably.' Marco grinned and spun her around.

Marco was a great dancer, and Liza was no slouch, and when the music ended she was naturally included in the group of his friends.

It was as she finished dancing with one of them over an hour later that she bumped into a hard male body. A strong arm wrapped around her waist and pulled her back a few steps.

'Enjoying yourself, Liza?' Nick's mocking drawl feathered across her cheek. 'Giving the young men a treat, I see.'

Spinning around out of his arms, she took a step back, and looked up and froze at the derision in his angry black eyes. But, pride coming to the fore, she flashed him a brilliant smile that did not reach her eyes. 'What did you expect, Nick? That I would stand at the side like a wallflower until you deigned to return?' she drawled sarcastically. 'Well, sorry, buster, but this is a party, and I intend to enjoy myself.' Once she would have been quelled by his attitude. Now she was just furious.

'Oh, I can see that.' His firm lips twisted in a sneer. 'The last boy you danced with had you hauled so close he was almost having sex with you. Not that I am surprised; you were sharing a suite with Henry Brown when I found you,' he drawled derisively.

The music had stopped and the last sentence fell like a stone in the muted conversations around them.

Liza spared him a bitter smile, and, jerking around, she pushed her way blindly through the crowd of people, tears prickling at the backs of her eyes. As humiliating moments went, that was a corker, and she had to get out of here. Now…

'Wait, Liza.' A large male hand grabbed her shoulder and spun her around. 'I'm sorry, I…' But she never heard him, as with a violent shrug she dislodged Nick's grip.

She was suddenly, furiously, magnificently angry at his undisguised contempt and his total humiliation of her. Why should she run away? He was the villain here. 'What for— so you can slag me off some more?' she prompted bitterly. 'I don't think so. You are a two-faced pig, you take what you want when you want it, and to hell with everyone else.' And she glanced up, her lovely face tense with strain and anger. Violent black eyes clashed with hers, and she shivered, her mouth running dry. She had gone too far…

A dark tide of red washed up over his high cheekbones. 'Are you through?' Nick demanded between gritted teeth. 'Trying to embarrass me in front of my whole family?'

Gathering what little will-power she had left, she plastered a smile on her face, and played the part of vamp he had obviously cast her in. She jutted her hip and put her hand on it, and, deliberately fluttering her long lashes up at him, she declared, 'What is sauce for the goose is sauce for the gander…big boy,' and then lifted her other hand and traced a slow path up his arm to rest on a hard bicep. 'But don't worry, I am out of here in the morning.'

Her mocking response set Nick back on his heels, and he had to fight down a twitch of reluctant amusement at her brave performance. He had never known such an infuriating bloody woman. Yet through the red haze of rage that had consumed him from the moment he saw her dancing with that handsome young man he suddenly realised she had given him the perfect solution to his problem…

'Depend on it.' He wrapped an arm around her waist and yanked her hard against him, and, dropping his head so only she could hear—they had been enough of a floorshow for one evening—he added, 'I'll see you off the premises myself.'

He had a ski-chalet in the mountains above Granada. It was the perfect place to keep her safe. 'I will even help you pack. But first you are going to dance with me, smile at me and try to behave like a lady for the rest of the evening. Understood?'

Her chin tilted fractionally. 'Perfectly.' And she bit her bottom lip hard to stop the sudden tremble. He could not have made it plainer what he thought of her. So what if it had been her suggestion to leave? In her heart of hearts she had not expected Nick to be quite so eager to see her go. He might have been overcome with lust last night and this morning but obviously he had very quickly had enough of her.

She held herself stiffly in his hold as they reached the dance floor. The music had changed to something slow, but she let her hands rest defensively on his strong arms as he urged her closer.

His dark head bent towards her and she felt his warm breath against her temple. 'No one will believe we are old friends if you persist in dancing like a puppet with a scowl on your face that would make a child cry at ten paces,' he mouthed against her skin and as he slipped lower his breath shivered over one earlobe.

Liza tried to resist the compelling power of his huge body, she stifled a sound in her throat, but it was no contest. In seconds she gave in and melted into the hard warmth of his embrace. They fitted together so well; one powerful thigh glided between her legs as he turned her slowly around the floor, and she was made shockingly aware of the strength of his arousal. She lifted startled eyes to his.

Nick saw the confusion in the darkening depths and for a moment she looked so young and acutely vulnerable. 'I think we have danced enough.' He loosened his hold on her slightly. 'It is time we did our duty and circulated a little.'

Nick had decided he would go along with the scenario she had painted. It fitted in with his plans ideally. As for the 'no sex in his mother's house', it would mean him keeping guard by the connecting door all night, rather than sharing her bed. But he could afford to wait with the prospect of sharing the ski-lodge with her tomorrow to look forward to.

Liza said nothing as Nick clasped her elbow and led her through the crowd, pausing here and there to speak to acquaintances, and with meticulous politeness introducing her as a friend of the family. She should have been pleased but instead she felt a deepening sense of dismay. That was compounded when they stopped to talk to Anna Menendez.

'Lovely party,' Liza said politely.

'I am so glad you are enjoying yourself, Liza, but don't let this son of mine monopolise you; there are some very handsome bachelors here tonight, and we can catch up on all the gossip tomorrow.'

'Sorry to disappoint, Mamma.' Nick wasn't sorry at all; he needed his mother encouraging Liza to flirt like a hole in the head, he thought furiously, but none of his anger showed in the dark eyes that met his mother's. 'But Liza has to leave tomorrow; she has to attend a conference she can't get out of. Isn't that right, Liza?' Nick demanded smoothly.

Liza took a deep breath, then released it slowly. She glanced at Nick; his dark eyes stared blandly back at her, with no sign of the incredible passion they had shared in the cold depths. He could not get rid of her fast enough. Forcing a smile to her face, Liza looked at Anna. 'Yes. Nick is right; I'm sorry, Anna, but I do have to go.'

Just for once she would have liked to ruffle Nick's colossal control and she added, 'I promised Henry…' and stopped, glancing back at Nick '…I mean, my boss…' her smile was a masterpiece of confident sensuality '…that I would return in time to go home with him.' She saw his dark eyes narrow, and felt his contempt right down to her bones, and she didn't care.

'Who is going where?' a husky voice interrupted.

'Sophia, darling.' Nick's delighted greeting knocked Liza's veneer of confidence for six, and she was forced to watch as Sophia, his supposedly ex-fiancée, slipped her arm through his and lifted her face for his kiss. Nick enthusiastically obliged.

'You remember Sophia, Liza.' His dark eyes lifted and he pinned Liza with a hard, challenging look.

Jealousy fierce and primitive lanced through her, but she managed to force a smile for the other woman. 'But of course. Hello, Sophia.'

'Hi; I never thought I would see you here again.' Sophia gave her a brief dismissive glance and then was whispering something coyly in Nick's ear.

Nick threw his arrogant head back and laughed out loud, and Liza felt as if she had been knifed in the gut. Obviously Nick was still very close to his ex-fiancée, and Liza felt about two inches tall.

'Excuse me,' she said to Anna, and turned on her heel. In minutes she was swallowed up in the crowd, and when she bumped into Marco she welcomed his easy-going attitude.

Held in Marco's arms as the band played a slow tune, she saw Nick dancing with Sophia. No, not dancing—glued together, they simply swayed to the music. Marco, catching the direction of her gaze, looked down at her. 'I saw you dancing with Nick before and I thought you and he might be an item.'

'Good heavens, no.' Liza pinned a bright smile on her face. 'We are old friends, nothing more.'

'Ah, I should have guessed when Sophia arrived and Nick grabbed you, the most beautiful girl in the room, he was probably trying to make her jealous.'

Liza looked up into the guileless young face of Marco. 'Why would Nick want to do that?' she asked, her stomach churning with nervous dread. 'I thought they broke up years ago.'

'I'll let you into a secret Anna told my mother, and she

told me. Nick is not quite the womaniser he seems. Apparently Nick met the love of his life years ago, and he thought she was his, but they parted and he has carried a torch for the girl ever since. Well, it has to be Sophia; it is common knowledge she left him when she finished university and got a job as a translator at the EU in Brussels. I think she liked the idea of a rich fiancé while she was a poor student in Madrid.'

'You think so?' Liza managed to murmur.

'Yes, she is a real career lady; no one has seen her at any family get-together since Nick's father died a few years ago. But it was common knowledge she had accepted the invitation to this party.'

As the music stopped Marco, with a hand at her elbow, led her to the side, and, turning, he chuckled, looking over her shoulder.

'I don't think they have noticed the music has stopped and Sophia is clinging to him like Velcro now, so it looks like making her jealous has finally worked for old Nick. The next big party here could be the wedding. The pair of them are both getting on a bit.'

Slowly Liza turned back and looked across the dance floor, and sure enough Nick was standing with his arms around Sophia, and she was smiling up into his face as if he was the only man in the world.

'Do you mind, Marco?' Liza excused herself to go to the rest room, fighting back the tears that threatened to fall. Hurt and anger raged in equal parts in her bruised and battered heart.

In a flash of blinding clarity she saw it all now. Her suspicions had been well-founded, but it had nothing to do with her wild idea of industrial espionage, and everything to do with the fact that Nick Menendez was an opportunist. He had bumped into Liza, and quite fancied her, and when his mother had called and reminded him to get back for the party he must have known he was going to see Sophia again, and saw an ideal way to make the love of his life jealous, and if he got a bit of sex on the side all the better. It was that basic.

Taking care to keep well away from Nick and Sophia, Liza finally found Anna and Thomas and his wife, and said her goodnights. Anna took her in her arms and kissed her. 'I may not see you in the morning, Liza; my old bones won't get out of bed so quickly any more. But please do try and come with your mother in March.'

The genuine affection in Anna's smile made Liza want to cry all the more. But she managed to control the tears until she made her way back through the brightly lit hacienda. She gave Manuel a weak smile as she passed the entrance to the kitchen, and a few moments later she carefully locked her bedroom door behind her.

Kicking off her shoes, she threw herself down on the bed and only then did she allow the tears to fall. How could she have been so gullible as to believe Nick had wanted her so badly he had to whisk her away with him? He had wanted her for one reason only, the most basic of human emotions—to make Sophia jealous.

Liza turned over and buried her head in the pillow, great sobs racking her slender body. She had been right to be suspicious all along. He still saw her as a tramp, because he thought nothing of using her for sex, and that was the cruellest cut of all. Choking on a sob, she felt her heart tear with grief, and she gave in to a paroxysm of weeping. Until finally she lay pale and still, her throat hoarse, and stared with sightless eyes at the ceiling, all cried out.

A long time later she sat up, and pressed her knuckles against her red-rimmed, swollen eyes. She and Nick had only ever been a childish dream; she should have left it that way. Now he was her worst nightmare, and, slipping off the bed, she headed straight for the shower.

What kind of idiot was she? she asked herself bitterly as she stood beneath the pounding spray. She had compromised her ideals in the first place by deciding to enjoy a holiday romance. Some joke! A one-night stand was all that had been on offer. She should have known when he got her into bed as soon as the damn plane took off!

Nick Menendez was an arrogant, unfeeling devil. He had told her years ago he liked extreme sports for the instant thrill, and kept looking for harder and harder challenges because he was easily bored. She had been a prize idiot for falling for his charismatic charm, and with a new determination in her eyes she scrubbed at her skin, determined to wash any memory of the man from her body and her thoughts.

CHAPTER EIGHT

LIZA finally gave up trying to sleep when she heard the muffled chimes of the clock in the hall strike six. At eight she was ready to leave, with her bag packed, her long hair divided into two neat braids and wearing denim jeans with a red shirt and denim jacket—she was dressed for travelling.

With one last look around the blue interior, she unlocked the bedroom door and, suitcase in hand, she left. Unable to resist, she glanced at the door to Nick's bedroom as she walked along the hall. It was wide open, and the bed was undisturbed. She closed her eyes briefly against the pain squeezing her heart, and quickly looked away.

Using her to make Sophia jealous had obviously worked for Nick, Liza thought bitterly. The hurt and humiliation were crushing, and she couldn't get out of the place fast enough. She was going to get the first plane back to Lanzarote; at least there she would be alone for a while, and free to lick her wounds in the privacy of her hotel suite. She wished like hell she had never left it and she didn't care if she had to sit all day at the airport; anything was better than staying here. She was angry at her own feeble-mindedness in wanting Nick. He had used her, and she despised the man...

With that thought in mind she marched into the kitchen and dumped her suitcase on the floor. Straightening up, she focused on Manuel busily preparing a coffee tray.

Manuel turned around. 'Señorita Liza, I was just about to bring you coffee.'

'Thank you, Manuel, but I am leaving as soon as possible. Would you please call me a taxi to take me to Malaga

Airport?' She walked past the kitchen table to where Manuel stood beside the preparation bench.

'But I will have a coffee while I wait.' Manuel filled a cup and handed it to her, and then stood hovering, as if he did not know what to do next. Spooning a big dollop of sugar in her cup—she needed the energy—Liza reminded him, 'The taxi, please, Manuel; I am in a hurry.'

'Yes, yes, of course.' He moved to where the telephone was suspended on the wall. 'For Malaga, you say.' He looked back at her with a frown. 'You are sure.'

'Yes, Manuel.'

'No, Manuel,' a deep voice commanded, 'a taxi will not be necessary. I will drive Liza into Malaga.'

Liza stiffened, anger and resentment simmering inside her along with a hollow feeling in her stomach that had nothing to do with hunger. So much for Nick's statement she was a welcome guest, she thought bitterly. He couldn't wait to see her leave, probably frightened in case she told Sophia what a love-rat he was.

With slow deliberation Liza sipped her cup of coffee to the dregs. Now all she had to do was face the dregs of her relationship with Nick. Placing the cup carefully down on the bench, she composed her features into a bland, socially acceptable mask.

Taking a deep, calming breath, she turned around. 'Good morning, Nick; that is very kind of you,' she said with determined brightness. 'But I would prefer a taxi.'

He was standing in the middle of the room, his magnificent body clad in black jeans and a white cashmere sweater, his legs slightly splayed and his thumbs tucked into the pockets of his trousers. He was all bristling male attitude, and the hard dark eyes that stared back at her held no hint of the intimacy they had shared, only a flash of irritation that she had declined his offer.

'Don't be ridiculous.'

Not only was she a slut but she was also ridiculous in his estimation. 'Thank you for that.' Her attempt at social politeness sank as the crushing weight of his betrayal sparked her anger. 'But I was trying to be reasonable. I would not dream of putting *you out* in any way,' she drawled sarcastically. She jerked her chin up, refusing to let him see how he had hurt her, and met his aloof gaze with stony eyes, at the same time thinking, what she would really like to do was knock the arrogant, deceitful devil *out flat*! But instead she added coolly, 'I'm sure you have much more important things to do with your time.' Sophia for one, she thought bitterly.

'But I insist, Liza. I brought you here; it is only good manners I assist you to depart, and I know what a stickler you are for good manners.'

A cold hand closed around her heart as she searched his handsome face. She saw his strong jawline harden, and the arrogant cynicism in his expression that said clearer than words that it was over. Pride alone made her step forward.

'In that case you won't mind getting my luggage,' she said with saccharine-sweetness and indicated her suitcase with a wave of her hand. 'I am in a hurry.'

'Not so great a hurry we can't have breakfast first, surely,' Nick prompted silkily. 'What time is your flight?'

She noticed there was no offer of the private jet. Why was she not surprised? He probably knew damn fine she had not booked a flight, he was simply being his usual sarcastic, superior self. 'I have no idea,' she said airily. 'I intend to wait on standby; the sooner I get back to Lanzarote the better.'

'Well, if you're sure I can't tempt you,' he drawled, the mockery in his eyes clear for Liza to see, 'to eat...' and scarlet colour stained her cheeks and she just knew the pig was laughing at her.

Five minutes later, seated in the passenger seat of a Land-Rover, Liza glanced at Nick as he started the motor. He was whistling! Whistling a catchy tune as if he had not a care in the world. But then, why would he? He was probably recalling his night in Sophia's bed.

The anger and resentment that had sustained her from the moment he walked into the kitchen this morning gave way to a gut-wrenching pain as an image of Nick naked with Sophia filled her mind, touching the other woman, kissing as he had kissed her... Turning her head, she looked out of the window at the countryside flying by without even seeing it.

What kind of idiot had she been to imagine that Nick would have the slightest interest in her, other than a quick roll in the hay? Maybe not so quick! But not much more than a one-night stand nevertheless.

Nick had hurt her at sixteen, his scathing comments had cut deep into her psyche, and she had deliberately denied her own sexuality for years. She had finally woken up to the fact after her broken engagement. She had realised she had dated Bob because he was no sexual threat; it wasn't surprising their one attempt at sex was a disaster, and she blamed herself for it. But the real blame lay with Nick, and, fool that she was, she had let him hurt her again almost a decade later. Was she never going to learn? He was Nick Menendez, a famously successful captain of industry, and an equally renowned womaniser.

In the sophisticated society he belonged to she had simply been a pleasant diversion for him, she realised bitterly. He had said he wanted her, but he did not trust or respect her, never had. Sex was all he wanted, to pass the time during a boring night flight, and until his long-time girlfriend turned up the next evening.

What on earth had she been thinking? Liza shook her head and slanted a glance at him with puzzled eyes, trying to fathom how one man could have so easily persuaded her to act so out of character. His handsome features were granite-hard and totally concentrated on the road ahead as he drove the Land-Rover way above the speed limit.

She had served her purpose, to make Sophia jealous and to provide a bit of casual sex on the side. She swallowed hard against the acid taste of shame that filled her mouth.

Her bitter gaze slid down to his hand on the gear stick, lean and strong, and she experienced a sudden rush of *déjà vu*.

Forty-eight hours ago she had been in the exact same position, but now she knew exactly what his hand felt like on every pore of her skin. She shuddered inwardly, her eyes misting with tears, and hastily she turned in her seat and looked out of the window again. Liza was emotionally exhausted, bone-deep tired—she had hardly slept in two nights—but she knew she had to get a grip on herself before they reached Malaga.

No way was she letting him see how much he had hurt her again...

As the road wound up high into the sierras Nick cast a sidelong glance at the sleeping Liza; her head had fallen against his arm, and a golden rope of hair lay on his chest. *Dios,* she looked about fifteen. What the hell was he doing? And he quickly turned his attention back to the twisting road.

Last night kidnapping Liza had seemed like a great idea. He was definitely losing his marbles... But not enough to turn around and head back towards Malaga Airport...

He had already lied to his friend Carl, and for a man who took pride in his honour he had behaved outrageously. He was a brilliant entrepreneur because he never invested in anything without a thorough investigation of the company and weighing up all the costs. He was good at dangerous sports, but only because he had the sense to take every reasonable safety precaution. His relationships with women were successful because he was generous, laid down the rules at the beginning and never got emotionally involved. He never acted on impulse...

Nick shook his dark head in bemusement. He had broken every one of his own tenets of behaviour, and why? Because of Liza; the sight, the feel, the touch of her affected him like no other woman. She turned his brilliant, decisive mind into mush.

'*Dios!*' He was halfway up a mountainside on his way to a secluded ski-chalet, with a sexy woman who might or might not be a criminal. Had he finally lost his mind? But a sidelong glance at the sleeping Liza and he had his answer. She was exquisite, and so innocent in sleep. His gaze moved over her beautiful face, her softly parted lips, and his chest heaved with a scarcely remembered emotion, a throwback to the past.

She looked just as she had at fifteen when they had taken the horses and gone on a picnic. Liza had been thrown from her horse, and he had jumped from his and cradled her head in his arms; her eyes were closed and for one terrible second he had thought she was dead. The same fear he had felt then Nick had felt again last night when Carl had told him two of the gang were still on the loose and could possibly target Liza.

It did not matter what she was or what she did, for some bizarre reason he was automatically programmed to protect her.

He manoeuvred the four-wheel-drive between a narrow cut in the cliff and brought it to a halt outside a log cabin. He leant back in the seat and glanced down as the golden head slipped forward, and Liza wriggled back against the constraints of the seat belt, and flung a hand across his lap.

Nick dragged in a sharp breath as his body tightened at her casual touch. She was going to wake up any second, and she was going to blow her top when she did. The thought was oddly exciting, but then everything about the mature Liza excited him, he wryly acknowledged. Even so, he was in no hurry to have the argument with her he knew must follow.

He looked out at the picturesque chalet nestled in the small clearing between the magnificent snow-covered mountains, and back to the sleeping woman. With Liza's head on his shoulder and hand on his thigh, the only sound in the silence was their own breathing. It was a moment to feed the soul…a moment of perfect peace…

* * *

Slowly Liza's eyes fluttered open; her hand was curved around a hard male thigh and her head pillowed against a comforting shoulder. She glanced sleepily up through the thick fringe of her lashes and blushed scarlet. Oh, my God! She had fallen asleep against Nick. Jerking up in the seat and avoiding looking at him, she blurted, 'Oh, good, we have arrived.'

'Glad you like it.' Nick unfastened his seat belt, pocketed the car keys and leapt to the ground. Any second now she was going to realise where she was, or wasn't! he thought with black humour quirking the corners of his mobile mouth, and he was taking no chances on her trying to drive off in a rage.

Glad! What was to like about an airport? And only then did Liza become aware of her surroundings. Her head swivelled ninety degrees each side, and, still not believing what she was seeing, she unfastened her seat belt and turned to look behind her; perhaps the airport… In the distance was a collection of buildings, and a ski lift! She turned back, her eyes widening to their fullest extent in shocked amazement.

Towering snow-clad mountains surrounded her, and a timber cabin and a couple of pine trees were directly in front of the Land-Rover. A sudden rush of air made her shiver and, as she glanced sideways, her stunned blue gaze clashed with narrowed black. Nick was holding open the door, his hand outstretched.

'Jump down and let's get the gear unloaded.'

'Jump down—are you mad? Have you taken leave of your senses? This isn't the airport. Where the hell are we?' She shot the questions in quick-fire succession, unable to believe her own eyes.

'Now, Liza, calm down,' Nick said smoothly, reaching for her.

Slapping his hands away, she yelled, 'Get your hands off me, you…you…crazy…' she yelled, shaking her head; she could not find an expletive bad enough to describe the sheer arrogance of the man. 'Calm down?' she screeched like a parrot. 'I will calm down when you get yourself back in this damn Land-Rover and drive me to the airport.'

Suddenly she was flying through the air and deposited on her feet, but held hard against Nick's mighty frame. She lashed out with fists and feet, anything she could use. 'Let go of me.' She struggled violently. 'I don't know what your game is but I am not playing it any more…I am going back,' she declared vehemently while her pulse rate accelerated off the scale in a mixture of fury and fatal attraction to the proximity of Nick's hard body.

'You aren't going anywhere,' Nick snarled as a rather good right landed on his jaw, and, swinging her off her feet, his arms tightened savagely around her, pinning hers to her side, his mouth crushing the furious retaliation she was about to utter back down her throat.

She tried to resist, tried to bite him, but in seconds, to her shame, she was succumbing to the burning excitement of his kiss, even as a tiny voice of reason told her she was courting pain by giving in to his powerful passion. 'Put me down,' she gasped when he allowed her to speak. 'I'm leaving.'

Nick merely laughed, and she shivered as he slowly lowered her down the long length of his muscular body. When her feet touched the ground she tried to pull free, but he was kissing her senseless again. She kicked his shin, anything she could reach, and when he finally ended the kiss she was breathless and mortified by her speedy surrender.

Liza drew in a very ragged breath, thought of Sophia and was incandescent with rage. 'You can stop that,' she yelled as Nick tightened his arms around her. 'Don't you dare kiss me again.'

Nick scanned the perfect oval of her face and noted the scarlet cheeks, his dark eyes narrowing perceptively. She wanted him, but she was mad as hell and he didn't blame her. 'Right at this moment I don't want to. I don't think my shins could stand it,' he answered with an insolent grin.

'Good, and get used to it. Because when I get back to civilisation I am going to charge you with kidnapping and you will probably end up in jail,' and as she spoke snow began to fall.

'You and I both, hmm,' Nick drawled, his dark eyes dancing with mocking amusement. 'Maybe we can share a cell.'

'Everything is a joke to you,' Liza said bitterly, so angry she didn't question his last comment. 'But you have gone too far this time. Take me to the airport immediately or I will make it my life's work to have you locked up, preferably in an insane asylum.'

Coming from Liza, that was too much for her would-be knight errant.

'Joke!' Nick exclaimed, fast losing his temper. 'Do you think I find this remotely funny, standing in a snowstorm arguing with you?' he opined hardly. 'I have had more fun skinning fish.' Her teeth chattered and he grasped her around her shoulders, pulling her tight into the warmth of his hard body. 'It's freezing. Come inside,' he commanded curtly.

'No, let go of me or I'll scream,' Liza cried, struggling to break free. Suddenly she was afraid; she glimpsed the icy resolve in Nick's long, hard glance, the barely controlled anger, and she had a horrible conviction once in the cabin she would never get away, and, worse, her traitorous body would not want to.

'Scream all you like, cause an avalanche, get us both killed,' Nick said grimly. 'Or let's get inside, and talk like two reasonable human beings.'

She was getting soaked, she was shivering and if she had given in to her impulse to scream... It didn't bear thinking about. But what were her options? A swift glance at the towering hills and snow-filled sky and she knew she didn't have any. Liza huffed, 'You...reasonable—that will be the day,' but let him lead her into the dry comfort of the cabin. She was a fool where Nick was concerned, but she was not foolish enough to risk pneumonia, or her life.

'I'll get a fire going; the kitchen is through there—you can put the kettle on,' Nick ordered with a gesture to one of two doors at the back of the room. 'The other door leads to the bedroom and bathroom, if you need it.' And, dropping to his knees in front of the open grate set in a large stone chimney breast, he began laying the fire.

Nick had tricked her into coming here—why, Liza had no idea, but that did not mean she had to obey his every command. If he wanted a hot drink he could get it himself, and she stood defiantly in the middle of the room.

Her angry gaze roamed over his crouched figure, white flakes of snow covered his head and as she watched they vanished into the blue-black hair, leaving it sleek and gleaming as a raven's wing. His shoulder blades flexed as he reached for some logs from the store box at the side of the hearth, and his tight buttocks strained the fabric of his jeans. Swallowing hard, Liza tore her gaze away from his powerful body—she was not going down that erotic route again—and looked around the room.

The simple living room revealed a black hide sofa and matching armchair, an occasional table with a few magazines, the top one featuring a figure leaping off a ski-jump—obviously winter-sports chronicles.

A solid wooden table, four chairs and a bookcase were the only other items of furniture. Liza wandered over to the table, picked up a magazine and settled herself in the armchair and contrived to appear relaxed. After the scuffle outside, she knew ranting and raving would get her nowhere. Cool reasoning was what she needed.

Nick was a complex man; highly respected in the business world, conservative where family were concerned, he projected an aloofness mingled with impeccable courtesy that most people found very charismatic, especially women. Yet he could also be hard and implacable, as he had been when he found her in the stable. Then again, yesterday, when he had hoisted her over his shoulder and carried her into the hacienda, he had unleashed a controlled violence that, as Liza recalled the scene now in the close confines of the cabin, made her shiver with inexplicable fear.

He had not become super-rich without taking risks, Liza knew, but kidnapping must be up there with one of the biggest. She didn't believe he would hurt her, not physically. As a child she had known him to be kind, considerate and with endless patience. Now she needed to exhibit some of that patience herself. He would have to tell her eventually why he had brought her here.

The fire crackled into life, flames casting eerie shadows on the cabin walls, and a moment later Liza watched as Nick stood up and took a step towards her, his broad frame vaguely threatening. 'Where are we?' she burst out, tilting her head back to look up into his coldly handsome face. Unfortunately patience was not one of her strong points. 'And why?'

For what seemed an age he surveyed her with dark, impenetrable eyes, his tall, strong body tense, then he thrust his hands in the pockets of his trousers. 'We are in my ski-cabin in the sierra an hour or so drive above Granada,' Nick responded with cool assurance. 'The ski resort is not far away, and I am hungry, so we can eat there or here; the choice is yours.'

'Eat. Is that your answer?' she asked incredulously. 'Do you ever think of anything except your appetite?'

An aristocratic black brow arched sardonically. 'You don't really want me to answer such a provocative question, Liza.'

'Yes—no...' she amended swiftly, agitation getting the better of her. 'But I do want to know why my winter holiday in the sun has left me freezing and stuck halfway up a mountain in the snow, with a man who could quite easily double as a maniac.'

Nick didn't move and she felt her breath quicken

slightly, and for a moment she almost believed there was a glimmer of regret in the dark eyes he had fixed on her with hypnotic, probing force. Then the moment was gone as he reached down and she flinched as he brushed his hand over her head.

'Your hair is wet with snow.'

'Hardly surprising,' she snorted and tossed her head, shaking off his hand. She was glad that she was sitting down as it made it easier to escape his too intent gaze, and she focused instead on the solid mass of his chest.

Nick studied Liza's down-bent head, her pale features, and felt a flicker of remorse and squared his broad shoulders. 'I know it is all my fault, Liza,' he confessed and, dropping to his haunches, he placed a hand on her shoulder, 'but I did it for us,' and with his other hand caught her chin and turned her head to face him. 'I wanted us to be alone together. I want you, and you said no sex in my mother's house. So...' He elevated one broad shoulder and rested dark, smouldering eyes on Liza's face.

'Do you honestly think I am stupid enough to fall for that line a second time?' Liza cried, about ready to explode with rage at the sheer cheek of the man. 'My God, you spent last night with Sophia—what kind of idiot do you take me for?' Shoving him hard, she leapt to her feet, gratified to see he had fallen on his bum, but couldn't help wishing it were his head.

Nick swore in Spanish and leapt to his feet, reaching out for her, but Liza took a quick step back. 'You really are a piece of work, Nick. Talk about double standards.' She studied him with contemptuous eyes. 'You think *I* am a slut... So what does that make you?' she derided with a shake of her head. 'Just get me out of here.' There was no point in arguing with the man.

'No.' Nick stilled, struck by the pained look in her eyes and appalled to realise she had taken words said in youthful anger years ago so much to heart. *Dios!* He was an unfeeling brute. 'Liza, I have never thought of you as anything other than a lovely girl.' He took a swift step toward her. 'And I never slept with Sophia.'

A lovely girl. For a second Liza almost believed him until she remembered where she was, and why, according to Nick? Because he wanted her alone! After what she had learned last night, she could not believe he was still prepared to lie through his teeth. Had she ever known Nick at all? she wondered bitterly.

She bit her lip and lowered her eyes; she had no illusions left. Loss of pride and humiliation lived inside her like a cancer, eating away at her self-respect, when she thought of how eager, how willingly she had fallen into his arms, her body warm and pliant to his every desire. Well, never again. She gritted her teeth and pushed the self-destructive feelings to the back of her mind. It had been a fleeting desire at best on his part, and it crossed her mind to wonder just how far the swine was prepared to go to achieve his own ends.

With that thought uppermost in her mind, Liza lifted her head and responded with an elegantly arched brow, cynicism evident. 'Never slept with your fiancée?'

'That was years ago!' Nick exclaimed with incredulously long-suffering masculine outrage at the vagrancy of the female. Any sane man would have concluded she was talking about last night. He could not do right for doing wrong in Liza's eyes, and he was getting mighty fed up with it.

'Last night for old time's sake, was it?' she prompted icily.

'There was no last night,' Nick snapped; as he knew to his cost, his rampant arousal had kept him up all night in both senses and it was this blue-eyed vixen's fault. He had spent the whole night seated on a chair by the connecting door to her room, keeping guard.

'Your bed wasn't slept in.' Liza realised with a sickening jolt she was in danger of revealing more than she wanted him to know. 'I happened to notice on my way out this morning.' She lifted a slight shoulder and dropped it again, feigning indifference.

Nick closed his eyes and breathed in deep and slow. She had turned his perfectly ordered life upside-down in a matter of days. He was furious with himself and furious with her, and lack of control was not a sensation he was accustomed to around women. But on the plus side he realised Liza was obviously jealous, which was something, and when he opened his eyes none of his emotions showed on his hard, handsome face.

'Why, Liza, I do believe you're jealous,' he drawled mockingly.

Liza went red then white and in a voice laced with pain she snarled, 'Of you, never,' her control suddenly breaking at his mocking assessment. 'Sophia is welcome to you.' Her voice cracked. 'You took up with me, made love...no, had sex with me simply to make her jealous. You probably dragged me up here because you're afraid I would tell her what a two-timing rat you are. That's it, isn't it?'

'Dios! You have some opinion of me if you think I would make love to two women in the same day,' Nick said grimly, and when he took a step forward into the light she could see faint lines of what looked like strain etched into his skin.

'My opinion does not matter, but God help Sophia when she marries you. I can almost feel sorry for her.'

'Married to Sophia, are you nuts?' Nick exclaimed and crossed the floor swiftly, grasping her chin before she could turn away, his breath warm against her skin, his eyes dark and shocked as he forced her to meet them. Of all the things he thought she might accuse him of when she discovered where they were...marrying Sophia was not one of them. He surveyed her with dark, impenetrable eyes, his tall, strong body tense, he saw the hurt she was trying valiantly to hide, and he felt like pond life. 'I don't know who has been filling your head with wild stories about Sophia, and me, but they are not true.'

'Don't give me that,' Liza said angrily. 'I always suspected you had an ulterior motive for bringing me to Spain, and the party.' She had tried living in a fool's paradise but it didn't work and now she decided to tell him the truth, she had nothing to lose...

'Marco told me everything. Apparently it's common knowledge you have been...' she couldn't say *in love* '...hankering after Sophia ever since she broke the engagement, and went to work in Brussels. And it was also common knowledge she was back in Spain for the first time in years and was attending the party. You used me to make her jealous and I will never forgive you for it. Now get me out of here.'

'No,' Nick said evenly. 'You have got it all wrong.' In this at least he could tell her the truth. 'Please, Liza, listen to me.'

'I have listened to you too damn much, which is why I am stuck in a cabin in the middle of nowhere instead of the cabin of a plane,' she declared hotly.

She was the most beautiful, infuriating, crazy, mixed-up lady he had ever known, and he couldn't help it—he laughed.

Incensed, Liza raised her hand and would have slapped his face but he caught her wrist. 'Calm down, Liza, and let me tell you the truth about my so-called engagement to Sophia. It was an engagement of convenience, nothing more.'

'Pull the other one,' Liza mocked, and frowned ferociously, determined not to listen to him.

Seeing her frown, Nick made a wry face. 'I am not proud of the fact, but at the time I got engaged you might remember my father had been diagnosed with cancer. His one wish was to see me settled with the firm and with a wife.'

She did remember her mother telling her that Señor Menendez was ill one Christmas, and the next summer Nick had been engaged.

'Work was no problem—I joined the firm, and I got engaged to Sophia to keep him happy. Sophia agreed because she wanted to go to university, and the engagement stopped her father grumbling about her wasting her time studying, when she should be finding a husband. I helped her out financially. It was a business agreement, nothing more, and it ended two months after my father died.'

'You expect me to believe that after last night?' Liza said flatly. But her own innate honesty forced her to admit if Marco had not told her the rumour about Nick and his unrequited love she probably would have believed him, because it had been a sudden engagement yet it had dragged on for three years, ending after the death of his father. The facts fitted. She was no longer sure what to believe, or who.

Nick stepped back and spread his hands wide. 'Why else would I tell you?' His mouth was sardonic. 'Think about it. If what you thought was true, and I was afraid you were going to speak to Sophia about us, it would make more sense to put you on the first plane out of Malaga.'

He always had an answer for everything, but he was right, damn him! Liza collapsed down on the sofa. 'Then why…' she demanded, shaking her head and looking confusedly around the small cabin '…why here?'

'Enough, let's stop this pointless argument,' Nick growled, his frustration getting the better of him, and, bending down, he flung a strong arm around her waist, lifted her bodily off the sofa and held her hard against him. 'All I am trying to do is protect your reputation.' And it was as near the truth as he dared tell her.

'By dragging me off to a cabin when I was on my way back to some sun in Lanzarote? Some protection!' Liza shot back derisively, and looked into his dark eyes, her own shooting sparks. Who the hell did he think he was? Hauling her around the countryside as if he was some mediaeval slave master, apparently for sex, without his precious family finding out. He wasn't protecting her, he was protecting himself…

'I wanted to be alone with you, and I had hoped you felt

the same,' Nick seethed and, swinging her up in his arms, he strode across the room and elbowed open a door. 'I am looking after you and that is the end of it.'

Imprisoned in his arms, Liza quailed at the barely leashed violence in his black eyes, and, looking away, her eyes collided with a massive white quilt-covered bed, and her temper soared. 'Forcibly carrying me into a bedroom…' she cried. 'You call that looking after—'

'Shut up,' Nick roared, dropping her onto the bed, and before she could move a muscle he was over her, his mouth covering hers in a savage, possessive kiss. 'This is our best line of communication,' he rasped against her swollen lips a long, savagely passionate moment later. 'The only one that need concern you. As for the rest, believe me, it is for your own good.'

CHAPTER NINE

'*FOR your own good.*' As a child Liza had hated that comment; it had invariably meant the opposite of what she wanted to do, and it sounded no better coming from Nick Menendez.

'No,' Liza yelped breathlessly, and was shocked by the darkening desire in his glittering eyes, felt it in the hard length of his body pressing her down into the mattress. 'You are no good for me or any woman,' she cried. 'And I wouldn't believe you if you were the last man on the planet.' She could not dismiss the notion that he had an ulterior motive for getting her on her own. If not Sophia, then maybe her original suspicion of industrial espionage was not such a wild idea.

Nick raised his head; he rolled off her, and flung an arm over his face. What the hell was he doing? She looked terrified.

Scrambling off the bed, Liza turned and glanced down at Nick, her face hot, another second and she would have been putty in his hands and the thought appalled her. She watched as his arm fell down to his side.

'It's all right, Liza, you have nothing to be afraid of. I have never forced a woman into bed, and I am not going to start with you.' His voice was flat and devoid of any emotion. 'I told you the truth about my relationship with Sophia, and as for wanting you,' a wry smile curved his mouth, 'that is certainly true. I knew that night on the plane that sexually we are extremely compatible. I don't think even you would argue with that.'

'No,' she said thickly. Liza felt confused, unable to move or think, and far too intensely aware of his long body reclining on the bed. She lowered her head and stared at her tightly linked hands, clasped together to stop them trembling.

'Good.' Nick rose in one fluid motion to stand towering over her. 'Then how about we start afresh?' He captured both her hands in his. 'Look at me, Liza,' he said quietly, and warily Liza lifted her head and met his dark eyes. 'We are two good friends on a skiing holiday.' He let go of her hands and tipped her chin with one long finger. 'That is all I ask. It can be a great holiday,' his eyes darkened perceptibly, 'or a fantastic holiday—the choice is yours; all you have to do is *ask*.'

She wouldn't have been human if she wasn't tempted but the wounds were still raw from the first time he had suggested a holiday. Amazingly Liza reminded herself it was only two days ago, and her emotions had been on a roller-coaster ride from ecstasy to agony ever since.

About to tell him no way, she changed her mind and took rapid mental stock. Nick was her first real lover, so it was hardly surprising doubt and suspicion plagued her. As for Sophia, she was inclined to believe Nick. He would hardly be here with her if he was madly in love with the other woman. Maybe his idea of being friends wasn't such a bad one; as for the rest, she was in charge... 'But why skiing?' She didn't realise she had spoken out loud.

'Because it is the national championships this week; some of my friends are taking part, and I love skiing.'

Liza's blue eyes widened to their fullest extent on his handsome face, her mouth falling open in shock at the sheepish expression in his incredible eyes. 'I don't believe it.'

'True, I swear, and you might even like watching.' And he grinned.

Liza had to fight down the insane desire to laugh. 'You are incorrigible.' She shook her head, her pigtails swinging. While she was thinking up wild scenarios as to why he had brought her here, it was nothing more than Nick being his usual arrogant self, doing what he wanted when he wanted. It was a classic Nick moment. 'But why drag me into it?'

'Do you really need to ask?' he queried with a sardonic smile.

She knew exactly what he meant and felt the tell-tale blush sweep up her face. Her throat tightened and her heart began to race.

Humorous dark eyes roamed blatantly over her shapely body. 'You know, for a beautiful, self-confident woman, you're incredibly unaware of your feminine power.'

'If I had any power,' she managed to snap back, 'I would not be stuck in a ski-cabin, but sunning myself on a beach.'

'I never thought.' Nick's dark brows drew together in a frown. 'You can't ski.'

'Yes, I can. I was a member of the ski club at university,' Liza swiftly contradicted him. But whether she could ski was not the point; then he smiled at her with that dazzling brilliance that took her breath away.

'Great.' He flicked his finger up under her chin. 'I'll go and make that hot drink.'

'Wait, I never said…' By the time she remembered what her point was he was gone and she was talking to herself.

Ten minutes later she was sitting at the kitchen table and Nick placed a cup of hot coffee in front of her. 'Get that down you, and then we will go to the lodge for lunch and get in an afternoon's skiing,' he declared as if her acceptance was a *fait accompli*, taking the seat opposite.

'But I can't—I have nothing to wear.' Liza cast him a fulminating glance, but was struck again by his sheer male magnificence. He looked gorgeous with his black hair ruffled, and his handsome face lit with enthusiasm for the sport ahead.

'How like a woman,' he drawled, a lazy smile curling his lips. 'But don't worry, there's a good shop at the lodge that will provide all you need.' Grasping her hand across the table, he stood up. 'Come on, let's go.'

Nick drove them the mile or so to the ski complex and

as they approached Liza's attention was caught by the swaying ski lift, and a bubble of excitement ignited inside her, for once not sexual...

'I haven't skied since I was at university,' she confided, her eyes roaming over the snow-covered slope dotted with people, eager to join them. 'I only hope I can remember how.' She smiled, glancing at Nick.

Nick slanted a look at her from beneath thick black lashes; her eyes were sparkling with anticipation, and her wide, excited smile illuminated her whole face. His breath snagged in his throat, and he brought the Land-Rover to a less than perfect halt outside the ski lodge.

In that moment he finally admitted what he had known deep down all along: Liza was no more a thief than he was. It wasn't in her nature. She was the same impulsive, easy to anger and easy to forgive, beautiful person she had always been from the first time he had set eyes on her at the tender age of eight, when she had cried and he had comforted her.

She was incapable of deceit. She hadn't a dishonest bone in her body. Her expressive features revealed every emotion with a dazzling honesty she could not hide, and when they made love she gave everything of herself with a wild generosity, a freedom of spirit not even the greatest actress in the world could aspire to.

Nick expelled a long breath, and leapt out of the Land-Rover. Even while trying to protect her, he had wanted to believe the worst of her. When had he become such a cynic? He moved around the Land-Rover, and, opening the passenger door, lifted a hand to her. 'Let me help you.'

Grinning, Liza took his outstretched hand and jumped down. 'Ever the gentleman,' she teased, and, glancing up, she stilled. His strong face was taut and his eyes were fixed on her with an intensity that shocked her.

'Nick.' His hand gripped hers so tightly it hurt. 'Nick, are you OK?'

Shaking his head, Nick let go of her hand. 'Fine.' He

slung a long arm around her slender shoulders and hugged her. He knew the truth now, always had, he thought wryly, and led her into the lodge.

'No, Nick,' Liza remonstrated as Nick asked the assistant to add an exquisite cashmere twin-set to the ski-suit and sweater she had already picked. 'I don't need anything else. Anyway, I have to be back in Lanzarote soon,' she reminded him. 'And at these prices I can't afford any more.'

Nick surveyed her with exasperated dark eyes. 'Don't be difficult, Liza.' He needed no reminding that their time together was limited, or that she wasn't the money-hungry thief he had thought. He felt bad enough as it was. 'I brought you here, and I am paying.'

Liza clashed with Nick's arrogant, intent gaze, and drew in a deep, steadying breath. 'It is not necessary.' And for a long moment their eyes locked, something indefinable passing between them.

'Maybe not for you, Liza, but it is for me. Let me do this for you, please,' Nick said softly.

Nick, less than his arrogant best and saying please! But what really stopped the refusal forming in Liza's throat was the unmistakable glimmer of vulnerability in the depths of his black eyes that she had never seen before. 'OK,' she agreed and was rewarded with a blinding smile, plus half an hour later enough clothes to keep her warm through a dozen winters.

Lunch was a thick meat soup with crusty bread, and Liza was surprised by the number of people who came up to speak to Nick. 'You seem to be well-known here,' she remarked as she ate the last mouthful of bread. 'I had no idea there was a ski resort of this size in Spain.' She looked out of the plate-glass window at the people dotted on the slopes. Nick had pointed out the different runs when they had sat down.

'The whole place was upgraded when the world championships were scheduled to be held here a few years back.'

A wry smile twisted his lips. 'Unfortunately it was the one year there was not enough snow.'

Liza laughed. 'How terrible.'

'For business, yes. But for the regular clientele all the new facilities are quite a godsend. There is a great viewing terrace above here with state-of-the-art telescopes if you want to watch the action close up.'

Later, covered head to toe in a red ski suit, Liza whooshed down the intermediate run at Nick's side for the third time. Reaching the bottom, breathless, her face glowing, she pulled off her goggles and looked up at Nick. He wasn't even breathing heavily. His black ski suit fitted him like a glove and she caught her breath at the magnificent figure he cut against the blinding white background. 'You don't have to stick with me, Nick; anyway, I have had enough. But I know you're itching to take the harder run.'

Shoving his glasses to the back of his head, Nick looked down into her eyes. 'Yes, I do, Liza.' Until the crooks were caught he was sticking to her side like glue, but he couldn't tell her that. And he would not put it past her to run away if the opportunity arose. 'You might disappear if I leave you on your own.' Liza saw he was deadly serious, and realised he thought she might just hitch a lift back to the nearest town, and his concern touched something deep inside her.

'I won't.' She placed a hand on his chest, and his fingers curled around hers.

Hearing her admission, Nick desperately wanted to take her in his arms. 'I believe you.' But he had virtually promised to wait until she asked, and she was worth waiting for. 'But it is time we left; you don't want to overdo the exercise on your first day.' Plus he needed to call Carl and find out if the two sailors had been caught yet.

Standing under the shower spray in the tiny bathroom, Liza hummed a popular tune as she rinsed the soap from her body. It had been a brilliant afternoon; she loved the skiing—it was so invigorating—and Nick had been the per-

fect companion…the hours had simply flown by. They had
eaten an early dinner at the resort and returned to the cabin
in companionable silence. Much better than sitting around
a beach, she concluded, and, drying herself off, she slipped
her nightie over her head and pulled on the short blue silk
gown she used for travelling. Walking back into the living
room, she smiled at Nick reclining in the armchair, a glass
of wine in his hand.

'Have you one of those for me?' She flopped down on
the sofa and yawned wildly. 'I think all this fresh air has
made me tired. I need a pick-me-up.' Her gaze strayed to
the logs blazing in the hearth and for a long moment she
was fascinated by the flickering flames; this was cosy, and
she let her head fall back against the soft cushions and
closed her eyes.

Nick stood in front of her, holding out a glass of cool
white wine. 'Liza.'

She opened her eyes, glanced up, smiled and took the
glass. 'The shower is all yours,' she murmured, for once
totally relaxed in his company.

'Thank you, ma'am.' He bowed, and she threw a cushion
at his head, and watched him disappear into the bathroom
with a grin on her face.

Liza finished the wine, and placed the glass on the table.
She wasn't sure what the future held but for now she was
going to live for the moment, and her holiday romance
might just work out after all, she thought lazily, her long
lashes flickering down over her eyes.

Nick walked out of the bathroom and stilled, transfixed
by the picture of Liza asleep on the sofa. His dark eyes
travelled from the shining mass of her hair to the soft curve
of her cheek, the lush bow of her mouth, and the outline
of her body beneath the soft silk wrap she was wearing.
He took a step forward, hungry to hold her, to kiss that
luscious mouth, to lose himself in that exquisite body. His
eyes darkened, and his body stirred. She was all his, he
thought possessively, and stopped.

Not yet. He tightened the towel around his hips, and quietly moved into the kitchen. His jacket hung on the back of the chair, and, fishing his mobile phone from the pocket, he punched in the relevant number. Five minutes later he switched it off, his hard face dark with frustrated anger; the news was not good. Carl had informed him the two men were still at liberty.

Nick walked silently back into the living room, and this time he did not stop.

Liza stirred restlessly and opened her eyes. 'Nick.' He was leaning over her, his black hair falling over his brow, and the only illumination in the room was coming from a small table-lamp.

'You were asleep on the sofa and I carried you into the bedroom.'

'Thank you,' Liza murmured, her lazy gaze wandering over him, and she realised he was naked except for a towel around his hips. She lifted her eyes and the austere lines of his face mesmerised her; she wanted to reach up and touch him. Some distant voice in her head told her no, but she lifted her hand and stroked it down the bold curve of his cheek. 'Where will you sleep?' she asked as her hand slipped to his broad shoulder, his dark, intent gaze colliding with hers. Her fingers flexed into the muscles of his shoulder and she heard his harsh intake of breath.

Nick groaned. 'The sofa.' He began to straighten.

'You don't have to,' she murmured, her other hand, palm flat, spreading over his heart, and she felt his chest expand.

'Do you know what you are saying?' Nick demanded hoarsely, his night-black eyes burning into hers.

'Yes, I…' and before she could finish his dark head dipped to claim her mouth in a deeply passionate kiss. His long body stretched out beside her, with one strong hand cupping the creamy fullness of her breast as he drew his thumb against her nipple causing her to shudder as it peaked instantly at his touch.

'You're sure?' Nick demanded when he finally allowed their lips to separate.

'Oh, yes,' she gasped, and a low moan escaped her as he trailed tiny kisses down her throat and travelled lower to tease her aching breast with his tongue before taking the rigid tip into his mouth. Liza felt as if every cell in her body was super-charged with electric tension and she looped her arms around his shoulders, straining against him.

Finally Nick lifted his head, his breathing harsh. 'The moment I saw you, Liza, I wanted you against all reason. Believe that if you believe nothing else,' he rasped with feeling.

She looked at him with desire-dazed eyes. 'I do.' Her gaze dropped to fix hungrily on his hard, sensual mouth as his head lowered and he claimed her lips with his own again.

'*Dios!* You are all woman, perfection.' Nick swept a lean, strong hand over a distended, rosy nipple, and lower to trace the line of waist and thigh. His dark head lowered, and his tongue circled her navel, sending a spasm of sensation through her, powerful enough to make her back arch from the bed.

He reared up and gave her a triumphant sensual smile full of hungry promise. 'We have all the time in the world, Liza.'

She wished it was true, and she sighed her pleasure as his powerfully muscle-toned body moved half over her and he was kissing her once more with a new urgency, a flaring hunger that fed the hunger she felt herself. His tongue delved deep into the moist interior of her mouth with a savage, mimicking need for the ultimate possession.

Welcoming the onslaught, she curved her hands instinctively into his shoulders, stroking the smooth bronzed skin, exploring every part of him with a rising excitement she made no attempt to hide. She heard him groan and felt the tiny tremors running through his powerful frame, and exalted in her power, but not for long.

Nick's black head moved lower against her body, his hands and mouth warm on her naked skin. Long fingers traced over her tense stomach and slid her quivering thighs apart.

A tidal wave of sensations hit her. She was all heat and tension that bordered on torture as he found the most intimate spot, and with hands and mouth tormented her. Shaking with an incredible excitement, she reached for him and begged, 'Please.' She could wait no longer. He was hard as steel and smooth as velvet, and she wanted him now...

Nick groaned, caught her hand and, muttering words she was too far gone to understand, he reared up and joined them with a thrusting passion, a driving determination to imprint his own indelible brand on her that swept Liza away on wave after wave of surging ecstasy. Out of control, he drove them wildly to a peak of passion that was almost pain before exploding in a mutual climax that left Liza breathless and quivering beneath him.

Nick rolled off her, and then hauled her close again in the curve of his strong arm, and for a long time the only sound was the heavy sound of their breathing. Their lovemaking had been so perfect, for once he was at a loss for the right words.

'You OK after all the skiing today, not sore?'

His question, coming out of nowhere at such a moment, was so ludicrous. Liza couldn't help it—she giggled... 'Yes. But why ask that now?' Her eyes sparkled with humour. 'What did you have in mind, naked down a mountain as an encore?'

Nick's firm lips parted in a broad grin that held a trace of relief. Liza never ceased to amaze him. 'For once you're ahead of me; the thought had never entered my head.' Lifting a finger, he circled her swollen lips, down her chin to the hollow in her throat. 'But, now it has, I will never be able to look at you on a ski run without envisaging you naked.' He dropped a gentle kiss on her nose. 'That could be very embarrassing for me.'

'Poor you,' Liza murmured. His strong body was relaxed against her, and she snuggled closer, throwing her arm across his broad chest. 'But it is your own fault.' She yawned widely. 'I was on my way back to Lanzarote. Skiing was your idea,' she teased because deep down, even after the most wonderful sex, she still didn't quite trust him.

Nick went very still. 'Are you disappointed?' he asked softly. 'Snow instead of sun?' Long fingers swept up to cup her cheek, and very gently his lips brushed against her own.

'No, no.' Liza sighed deliciously. 'I think I can stand a lot more of this, and the skiing, naked or otherwise,' she teased.

'Good, and I think you should pay for my future discomfort on the slopes,' Nick drawled huskily and kissed her. And she did…

Dressed in smart wool trousers and a soft pink cashmere sweater, Liza washed the smudge of lipstick off her finger, dried her hands and placed the towel back on the rail. She was ready except for her shoes. She cast one last glance at her reflection in the mirror. She had heard women described as glowing, but had never seen it herself until today. That's what a good man can do for you, gal! she thought, and grinned.

The past five days had been magical. They had skied, made love and simply had fun. Nick had tried to teach her snow-boarding without much success. And for the first time she had seen him with close friends—two of the slalom racers and their wives. Nick was too controlled to reveal much emotion but last night they had all dined together and he had been totally relaxed, laughing and sharing what were obviously in-jokes, and reminiscences forged over a number of years. It was a side of him she had never seen before. She had never felt so close to another human being in her life. He enthralled and enraged her but she wouldn't have him any other way.

Barefoot, she padded out of the bathroom and into the kitchen. Nick was standing by the window, his back to her, talking on his mobile. She allowed herself a moment to admire his behind in the tight black ski-pants.

'Really, there is no need for you to come to Spain. I mean it, Carl, no.' Nick switched off the phone.

'Ah, the mysterious Mr Carl Dalk,' Liza chuckled, walking towards him.

Nick spun around, his dark eyes narrowing intently on her face. 'How much did you hear?'

Liza stopped, surprised by his quick question, and looked up at him. 'Nothing much, just that there was no need for him to come here, or something like that.'

'Good.' Nick squared his broad shoulders but avoided meeting her eyes. He slipped the mobile in his jacket pocket.

'Why? Don't you want me to meet your friend?' Liza asked lightly. 'According to your mum, he is very handsome and very wealthy—jealous are you?' she joked.

'Don't be ridiculous,' Nick snapped back. He should be happy; the news was good. Carl had just informed him that the panic was over. The two men had been picked up at the airport last night trying to board a flight to Malaga, and were safely under lock and key. Daidolas had passed the valuation on to a middleman in Morocco. The top investigator from Nick's agency was keeping tabs on the Moroccan. Carl and the police had the rest covered. Now all they had to do was wait for the approach to the insurers and set up the transfer. With Liza's information that Brown was returning to the island a week today, it was almost certain that would be the day for the hand-over.

Nick no longer had a reason to keep Liza at his side twenty-four hours a day; she was safe for the moment. He could take part in the para-skiing competition, so why wasn't he thrilled?

'I was only joking,' Liza said placatingly, breaking the rather tense silence and wondering what had happened to change his mood from the eager lover of an hour ago, to the stern-faced man in front of her.

'It wasn't funny; you don't know Carl,' Nick said bluntly, 'and if you have any sense you will forget you ever heard his name.' Liza was not out of the woods yet, as far as the criminal investigation went and she might still be questioned, and the less she knew about anything or anyone the better... 'Understand.'

No, Liza did not understand. But she reached out to him, one small hand catching his arm, the other she placed on his chest and lifted her brilliant eyes to his darkly handsome face. 'I understand you seem a bit uptight, and you need to relax,' she said softly. But the light in her eyes faded as he flinched and drew back from her.

'Don't waste your time—we've run out of condoms,' he informed her with a bluntness that shocked Liza to the core. 'I'll get some at the lodge later.'

Dazedly she looked at him; he was so cool and matter-of-fact she was painfully reminded of exactly what Nick wanted from their affair: sex; he had never pretended otherwise. Of course, he was right to take precautions, she knew, but she bitterly resented the implication that just because she touched him it had to lead to sex.

'You do surprise me, Nick.' It had taken a few moments but now she was back in control and she was coldly angry. 'I would have thought a man like you would have an inexhaustible supply,' she said sarcastically, and watched his head jerk back.

'A man like me?' he said with a raised brow. 'I believe in protecting my lover and myself, but can your past lovers say the same?'

His insinuation was like a red rag to a bull. He was frightened of catching something off *her*! 'You've got a nerve. I bet you have a little black book that would rival the Encyclopaedia Britannica,' she shot back.

'Oh, Liza, come on, you were no virgin and I don't care how many lovers you have had. But if you are on the Pill I am perfectly happy to forget about the condoms.' And he had the audacity to smile, like a man who thought he should be thanked for being so generous.

'I am not on the Pill, and I have only ever had one other lover.' She was incensed by his callous comment about 'lovers' in the plural.

'And who was that?' Nick asked cynically. 'Henry Brown?'

'No way—are you crazy? He is my boss and he is married.' She was insulted that he could even think she would sleep with a married man, and she could not understand how a comment about a telephone call had led to a discussion on her sex life or previous lack of one.

'Then who?' Nick asked, relief flooding through him at her denial; the thought of Liza with Brown had been anathema to him.

'Not that it is any of your business, but it was my fiancé,' she told him and then wondered, was she really so besotted with Nick she actually saw his interest in her past love life as a sign of real interest in her?

'You were engaged; for how long?' Nick looked at her in astonishment. He had never heard that bit of information from his mother, he was sure.

'Three days,' Liza admitted drily. 'The first time we made love it was a disaster, so we didn't do it again. In fact, I thought I was frigid.' She saw the expression of amazement on his face, and blushed.

'You are joking!' he exclaimed and laughed out loud.

Of course, to a man with his sexual history she must sound like an idiot, and quite suddenly she was furious. 'Very funny, ha ha! But no, I am not joking. In fact, I should be thanking you for showing me I am not frigid. At least now when we part I will have no fear of dating dozens of men.' And with that broadside she busied herself clearing the dishes to the sink.

Nick believed her; he had thought the first time they made love she was a little shy, shocked by her own response, and he was secretly delighted that he was the one to teach her the wonder of sex. But she was a fast learner, and he was damned if he wanted her trying out her new-found sexual prowess on anyone but himself. The thought brought him up cold.

'I have to go. I want to watch the first slalom race,' Nick said brusquely. 'So if you want a lift to the lodge you'd better hurry up.' He looked at his watch. 'I'll give you five minutes, but you can stay here for the day if you like, have a rest.'

'What did you say?' Liza spun around, blue eyes blazing. *Stay here...if she liked...* When had he ever cared what she wanted? Liza thought mutinously. She searched his strikingly handsome features for some reassurance, but his face was expressionless.

Not meeting her eyes, he strode out through the door, shouting over his shoulder, 'Five minutes.'

Swerving to miss a young child, Liza ended the run on her back. That was it, she had had enough and, struggling upright, she headed for the lodge. Nick had parted company with her as soon as they arrived on the slopes, with a brief comment that he wanted to tackle something different. On her own for the first time in a week, she was very quickly bored, going up and down the same route.

She stacked her skis against the wall, and after changing out of her ski suit she headed for the viewing terrace; maybe she could pick out Nick. She was surprised at the amount of people that were around; still, she managed to get one of the telescopes and scanned all the ski runs, but couldn't see Nick.

She heard a commotion behind her and turned around. Funny, all the other telescopes had been turned around, and then she saw what was causing the excitement. 'Oh, my

God! What are they doing?' she asked, and the man next to her answered.

'Ah, you mean the crazy para-skiing.' And he swiftly adjusted her telescope for her towards the high mountain range behind the ski runs. 'Look up there, *señorita*. They leap off the peak and they are lucky not to break their necks.' He shook his head and laughed. 'Extreme sports.' He shrugged. 'Plain loco.'

Focusing on the mountain, Liza let out a horrified gasp as she spotted the distinctive figure of Nick dressed in black, and as she watched he took off, a black parachute with the red emblem of the Timanfaye devil emblazoned across sailing above him. He soared and dipped down the mountainside, his great body twisting and turning as he skimmed rocky outcrops and jumped off cliffs with a total disregard for life and limb.

All the colour drained from her face, her heart leapt into her throat as his body flew through the air, and she expected any second he would be smashed against a cliff. She watched until his distinctive chute finally vanished behind another mountain.

Turning away, her legs trembling, she went inside and straight down to the bar, ordered a large Scotch, and, crossing to a quiet corner, she slumped down into an armchair and drank the whisky down in one go.

Her heart was pounding like a drum in her chest, and she felt sick. Sick with fear, not for herself, but for Nick. A vivid mental picture of his magnificent body broken and bloody on the white snow flashed in her mind, and she groaned. Oh, God, why did he do such things? What made a sane man risk his life over and over again in the name of fun? She wouldn't call it a sport, it was sheer reckless, macho bravado, and she hated the very thought of Nick even contemplating taking part, never mind actually doing it.

Liza's teeth clenched, rage sweeping through every cell

in her body. She would kill him when she got her hands on him, if he had not killed himself first...

The sheer stupidity of her angry reaction hit her, and with it came the knowledge that she had been trying to deny all week, that she was falling in love with him...

No, that way lay heartbreak, as sure as night followed day. She had been terrified watching Nick this afternoon, sick to her stomach. She could imagine the agony all too easily of loving such a man. Wondering every time he took part in such events if he would ever come back.

She already had a taste of the pain, wondering now if he was safe, and she hated it. She had thought she was in love once with Bob, and that had been a disaster. No way was she going down the same route again. Rising to her feet, Liza ran her hands through her glorious hair, her face pale but determined as she walked towards the exit.

Now she knew why Nick had been edgy this morning. He must have been high on adrenaline, tension stretched to breaking point as he thought of the event ahead. No wonder he had not really wanted her to come with him. He had not even told her what he was going to do...

Dinner was a raucous affair. Liza sat quietly at Nick's side as he and his friends discussed every twist and turn of their monumental folly as far as Liza was concerned.

Much later in the dark comfort of the big bed, Nick made love to her with a wild, hungry passion. He moved inside her, and groaned something she could not hear, his eyes blazing in a face that was tense and drawn in a rictus of desire.

She kissed him then and he drove her higher, sensation building on sensation until she was mindless, aware only of the strength of him possessing her utterly, and she cried out his name and climaxed, and climaxed again, and felt his great body shuddering over her, before collapsing on top of her.

Nick rolled onto his back, taking her with him, and she laid her head against his chest as his pounding heart slowed beneath her cheek and returned to normal. His long arm wrapped around her waist and he squeezed gently.

'You never cease to amaze me, Liza. I think I've told you that before,' he said softly. 'You're a woman in a million.' His hand gently brushed back the tumbled mass of hair from her brow. 'I was sure you would be mad today when you discovered what I was doing, and yet it never fazed you at all. Thank you.'

Turning slightly, Liza looked up into his dark eyes, saw the warmth and, yes, affection, and she had to summon all her inner strength to say what she knew she must. 'No need to thank me, Nick; if you want to kill yourself that is your prerogative. I am out of here next Friday and back to work.' She felt the slight tension in his body. 'Holiday over.'

'Then we'd better not waste time talking.' And she was on her back and Nick claimed her mouth with his.

Liza crouched down to remove her skis and paused for a moment. She could see the rise and dip of the mountains, the snow, dazzling to the eyes in the midday sun, and she blinked back a tear.

They were leaving for the airport in an hour, and to head back to Lanzarote. She should really have left early this morning but Nick had persuaded her to stay for one last run, convincing her that he would get her back in time for the gala dinner. Not that she needed much convincing…

'What's wrong?' Nick asked, and, removing his sunglasses, he crouched down beside her. 'Skis stuck?'

Liza looked at him, the concern in the depths of his glorious dark eyes making her heart shake. It never stopped, the hunger, the need for him, and she shook her head. 'Nothing.' And she rose to her feet before he could see the moisture in her eyes. 'We'd better get changed and get going.' It was the end of an idyllic holiday and she had vowed to herself she would not ask for more. 'I do have to be in Lanzarote tonight.'

Nick straightened to his feet. 'Yes,' he agreed, tension riding him. It was nearly over but not quite.

They entered the building together, but not touching, and headed for the changing rooms. Liza stopped and tilted her head back to look up at Nick, the darkness of indoors after the dazzling light outside blinding her for a moment. 'Where shall we meet?'

'Upstairs on the balcony,' Nick responded, 'but there is no hurry; take your time getting ready,' he told her, and, her eyes adjusting to the shadow, Liza studied his darkly handsome face. His jaw was set, his expression cold and remote. He was already withdrawing from her. She could sense it, had done all morning if she was honest. But then she had been doing the same since last week, or trying to, determined not to fall in love with him.

Involuntarily she lifted her hand to touch his cheek, but stopped, and instead she brushed back a few stray locks of hair from her face. 'Right, OK.' She dived into the changing room, tears blinding her.

Roughly she wiped the tears from her eyes. She was not going to cry. It had been great. She had had her holiday romance and that was enough. In a few hours she needed never see him again.

He had said to take her time, but suddenly Liza just wanted the parting over with as quickly as possible. She stripped off her ski clothes, didn't bother with a shower, and, pulling on the denim jeans she had arrived in, she slipped on a roll-neck sweater in blue and added the denim jacket. The rest of her gear was already packed and in the Land-Rover.

Tense wasn't the word. Nick walked out onto the balcony, and flicked on his mobile phone. He had spoken to Carl early this morning when Liza was sleeping, and knew Brown's yacht had just berthed in the marina at Teguise. He also knew the transfer of cash and diamonds had been set for ten-thirty at a remote spot in the Timanfaya National

Park. What Nick was hoping for was that whoever made the transfer would head straight back to Henry Brown and they would all be picked up.

He glanced at the Rolex on his wrist—it was almost one—and waited impatiently while the telephone rang. He prayed Carl would have the information he wanted.

He had talked Liza out of leaving this morning but he couldn't delay her much longer. Not that it mattered now. He had never had any intention of taking her back to Lanzarote; once on board his jet, they were heading for England, a two-and-a-half-hour flight. By the time Liza realised and they landed, she wouldn't have time to go back to the island.

Liza was still suspicious. He had sensed a wariness in her the last week and she had asked him again last night how he knew her boss when he was arranging their departure for today. He had changed the subject by making love to her, but she would not be diverted forever that way.

His lips twitched in a fleeting smile; though he would love to try. *Dios!* but she was good! The blunt thought made him frown. Good wasn't the word to describe how he felt when he touched her naked body, felt the heat of her when he knelt in the delta of her thighs, the heightened sensations that made him tremble like a teenager with his first girl. Nick groaned, he ached with the need she aroused in him.

When this call was over and he had arranged to keep Liza in the clear…that was if Carl ever answered; he frowned at the continuing ringing tone. He was going to tell her the truth. His honour would not allow him to do less, and then if she was still willing they could continue their relationship with no secrets…totally open.

'Carl here.'

'What's happened?' Nick demanded. 'Have you picked Brown up yet?'

'Mission accomplished.' Carl's voice rang with triumph. 'Would you believe Brown called at Daidolas's when he left the yacht to go to his hotel? He couldn't resist checking the diamonds again before they were handed over to the courier for the exchange, and we have the whole thing on video. Brown was getting far too complacent—he should have remembered third time lucky, or unlucky in his case. The courier arrived at the meeting place and we trailed him straight back to Brown at his hotel. We picked them both up along with Daidolas.'

'Great!' Nick exclaimed.

Liza reached the top step that led out through a double door onto the balcony when she heard Nick's voice, and wondered who he was talking to. She froze at the mention of her boss's name.

Totally unaware of Liza's presence, Nick carried on. 'So we finally got that thieving bastard Henry Brown. I hope they lock him up for years. Congratulations.'

'With a lot of help from you, Nick. Your questioning of the girl and keeping tabs on her was brilliant. But when are you bringing her back?'

'Keeping tabs on Liza was no hardship,' Nick chuckled, the relief he felt that the whole thing was almost over immense. 'But I wanted to talk to you about her.' He hitched a hip onto the balcony rail, and let his glance roam over the view before him, searching for the right words. 'I know we thought Liza was involved with Brown in the theft of the diamonds when she delivered them for him. Now you have Brown under lock and key in a Spanish jail with the rest of them...'

Liza listened with mounting horror as Nick's deep, melodious voice spelt out exactly what he thought of her. A diamond thief! She tuned out the rest—she didn't need to hear how he was going to deliver her to jail.

Suddenly everything was crystal-clear in her shocked mind, and she had never felt so shamed and humiliated in her whole life, and she had only herself to blame.

All Nick's questions about her job and her boss and her

movements took on a sinister slant. As soon as she'd met up with Anna, Liza had been suspicious of Nick's motives for taking her to Spain and she had been right all along about him knowing the name Henry Brown without her telling him. He had been having him followed.

But she had let herself be convinced that it was Nick's overwhelming desire for her that had driven him to the deception. Then when she found herself at the ski-cabin instead of an airport she had fallen for his overwhelming-desire routine a second time.

What kind of sex-starved idiot did that make her, when she was stupid enough to believe his double deception? The bitter truth was all the time he had been keeping her under surveillance because he thought she was a jewel thief.

Liza felt like screaming her anguish at the mountains. She had been braving herself to say a sophisticated goodbye at the end of a holiday romance, and the lying, deceitful... The words escaped her.

Fury as ferocious as it was primitive swamped her. She wanted to scratch Nick's lying eyes out, and in a red haze of rage she dashed towards him.

CHAPTER TEN

'WHAT the hell...?' Nick exclaimed. He caught a brief glimpse of Liza as a small clenched fist caught him on his jaw and sent him reeling backwards. He made a wild grab for the rail and just stopped himself plunging thirty feet to the snow-covered ground below.

'You bastard!' she yelled. She saw his head jerk back and his great body sway, and stopped dead, paralysed by fear at where her anger had almost led. She might have killed him. Frozen in shock, she simply stared as he leapt towards her. Two strong hands grabbed her by the shoulders and his black eyes, leaping with fury, clashed with hers. 'I'm—' sorry; the word formed in her mouth but he cut her off.

'Have you taken leave of your senses, you stupid bitch?' he roared. 'You could have killed me.'

It was the *stupid bitch* that did it. Snapped out of her frozen horror, she forgot any intention of apologising. Flinging back her head, she met his furious gaze with bitter, angry eyes. 'Pity I didn't,' she snapped, ruthlessly banking down the pain that she could feel twisting inside her. He had lied and cheated once too often, hurt her for the last time, and fiercely she held his black gaze as the tension stretched between them, determined not to look away, not to show any sign of weakness. She had been weak where Nick was concerned for far too long.

'What did you say?' Nick hissed with sibilant softness, finally breaking the lengthening silence, and it was only the clenched muscles of his implacable face, and the fingers digging into her shoulders that betrayed his barely contained fury.

'You heard,' Liza said, her voice toneless. 'But don't worry, Nick, I will never touch you again. It is quite enough for me to be known as a thief, without adding murderer.'

Nick's hand moved from one shoulder and grasped her chin, roughly tilting her face up to within inches of his own, his breath warm against her skin, his eyes dark and violent. 'You nearly kill me and that is all you have got to say,' he snarled. '*Dios mio!* You are unbelievable. You overheard something you didn't like and lashed out without even waiting for an explanation.'

'Another explanation! Along the lines you were overcome with passion, you wanted me alone,' Liza drawled sarcastically. She could feel the icy shock at what she had overheard dissipating, and she knew the pain was waiting for her, but she still managed to continue. 'Try—I can take care of Liza the thief, while your friend has my boss flung in jail.'

'No,' Nick drew a deep, exasperated breath, 'it wasn't like that.'

Through the mounting pain in her heart Liza stared at him. 'The day we met you were looking for me; it wasn't an accidental meeting at all?' she realised suddenly, her mind suddenly clear as a bell. 'You asked me about my work, and I happily told you everything.' She shook her blonde head, her blue eyes glacial. 'I should have known you were up to something. You hadn't spoken to me in years. You always thought I was a slut, but it never entered my head you thought I was a thief as well.'

'Liza.'

She wrenched free of him. 'Don't bother denying it, Nick.' She glared at him bitterly. 'Just tell me, how could you bear to make love to me, thinking as you do?' And, without waiting for an answer, 'No, don't bother.' She raised a hand to his face palm towards him. 'For the Spanish Stud, it was probably an added thrill for your jaded palate to seduce me.'

'I never seduced you,' Nick began darkly, 'and I regret you overheard something that upset you, but—'

'But you did think I was a thief,' Liza prompted and saw the dark colour sweeping up under his skin. He was fuming, but he could not deny it.

'You don't understand,' Nick grated, his glittering eyes raking over her. 'I can explain.' He had lied to his best friend to protect this woman, and what had he got in return? A near-death experience and an aching jaw, and now Liza was looking at him with loathing.

'There is nothing to explain; I already know it all.' He had seduced her with his sophisticated expertise and she had let him, while all the time he had thought her a thief. She didn't need the details, all she needed was to get away before the pain swamped her and she broke down in tears. 'You are a lying, lecherous apology for a man and I never want to set eyes on you again in my life.' Spinning on her heel, she dashed headlong for the stairs.

Reaching the ground-floor exit, Liza halted, her eyes aching with unshed tears and bile rising in her throat in a tide of self-loathing as she remembered how she had been with Nick—pathetically eager to explore every erotic nuance of sex, glorying in his body, touching him, tasting him, and all the time he must have been laughing at her...

She recalled that very first day Nick had taken her to Spain and to his bed, and she had let him, welcomed him with open arms. For the first time in years she had met a man who could make her break the tight bonds of restraint around her emotions. Knowing he was not into commitment, she had told herself she was mature, confident enough to handle a sexual affair. A holiday romance.

Now she realised Nick hadn't even been offering that. His real agenda had been much more sinister; he had been quizzing her for information while keeping her under surveillance for his friend Carl Dalk. She thought of the times he had dismissed her suspicions as nothing, but she realised now she should have trusted her instincts. She had always known he thought she was a tramp; it wasn't much of a jump to think her a thief as well, and act as her jailer.

Not any more…Liza thought, her anger boiling up again. What gave Nick Menendez the right to act as judge and jury on her character? She straightened her shoulders, and stepped out into the brilliant afternoon sun. Nick was a ruthless devil and she should have remembered that instead of being blinded by sex.

She took a few deep, steadying breaths and looked around. She saw the Land-Rover; her luggage was in there, but she didn't give a damn. She would hitch a lift if she could; she was getting out of here now. She had her passport and credit cards—she didn't need anything else.

'Wait, Liza.' Nick's strong hand closed around her arm, and furiously she tried to wrench free, but he held her firm. 'This is Señor Lancio.' Only then did she notice the short, stocky man at his side. 'I have arranged for him to drive you to the airport; my plane is waiting, as you know, and the pilot has instructions to take you straight to your destination.' Urging her towards the Land-Rover, he stopped to allow Señor Lancio to open the passenger door, then he let go of her arm. 'Be my guest.'

'No, thanks, I have been your guest once too often already,' Liza slashed back, her blazing blue eyes clashing with black, 'and I don't like what it entails.'

'You have nothing to worry about. As you requested, I will not subject you to my presence any longer.'

Liza looked at the vehicle, saw Señor Lancio get in the driving seat and start the engine. She looked back at Nick. What the hell? At least she would get away from him quicker this way and climbed in. She fastened the safety belt and stared straight ahead as Señor Lancio manoeuvred the vehicle out of the car park, making a mental note not to fall asleep like last time, or she might end up in Timbuktu!

* * *

Monday morning Liza sat on the tube trundling its way under the city of London, and wondered if the last two weeks had been a dream or a nightmare. She guessed she would soon find out.

A vivid image of Nick Menendez the last time she had seen him filled her mind. He was standing by the Land-Rover, his handsome face as hard as granite, his black eyes frozen as they met hers.

Thinking about it now, Liza closed her eyes briefly. Nick had still had the last laugh, damn him! She had boarded the private plane, and it was only when the plane landed she'd realised she was not in Lanzarote… He had sent her back to London.

Back in her flat, she had tried to ring the hotel and discover if Henry Brown was there. But it had proved a fruitless exercise—they refused to discuss guests over the telephone—and when she had pointed out she was supposedly a guest herself, for some inexplicable reason there was no trace of her ever having signed in.

She had spent the whole weekend locked in her apartment, alternating between tears for a love that had never been and fury at the man who had done this to her. In her saner moments she had paced the floor, trying to fathom out why she had been gullible enough to accept Henry Brown's glib offer of a holiday.

Even worse—why had she delivered the package for him? It must have been the diamonds Nick was talking about to his friend; she realised that much, but the ramifications of her action filled her with terror. If Henry Brown was guilty of diamond smuggling then she was without doubt an accomplice. She could declare her innocence until she was blue in the face, but actions spoke louder than words, and years in a Spanish jail loomed large in her nightmares.

As the tube came to a halt at her stop Liza got up and pushed her way through the crowd of commuters and out onto the street. She pulled the collar of her coat up around her neck and, with head bent against the freezing wind, she set off walking towards the office, not sure what she would find when she got there, but pride and belief in her own innocence made her hold her head high as she walked into the reception area.

With no 'hello' or 'good morning', the pretty, dark-haired receptionist looked at Liza with barely concealed curiosity in her eyes. 'Mr Stubbs is back and he is waiting for you in the boardroom.'

With a brief nod of her head in acceptance, Liza made her way to the boardroom. Her old boss back from retirement simply confirmed her worst fears. So it was with a fast-beating heart she walked into the oak-panelled room, and closed the door behind her.

'Liza, Liza, my dear.' Mr Stubbs immediately crossed to take her arm. 'Come along and sit down.' He pulled out a chair at the long, polished table, and Liza was glad to sit down; her legs felt like rubber. Panic was beginning to take root in her mind.

Mr Stubbs sat at the head of the table, and took her hand in his. 'Thank goodness you are back safely. I blame myself for encouraging you to work for that bounder Brown when I retired. He pulled the wool over everyone's eyes. Not content with making a very good income with my company, he had to go and freelance as a diamond thief. What is the City coming to when thieving men like that can flourish? But thank God he is caught, and thanks to you our firm will not be involved.'

Her mouth fell open like a goldfish. Mr Stubbs was thanking her…

'You obviously have friends in very high places.'

'Me…?' Liza breathed, a hand to her chest. 'I don't understand.' She shook her head in bemusement; she had half expected a policeman to be waiting for her, not a grinning Mr Stubbs. 'What has happened?' she asked, and Mr Stubbs proceeded to tell her in detail.

Apparently Mr Stubbs had been approached on Friday afternoon by the Spanish Embassy and within the hour a detective from the Spanish police was interviewing him. He was informed his top executive Henry Brown was a diamond thief, and he had used the company expense account to hire yachts to transport the diamonds with the help of a motley crew, now all in custody.

Mr Stubbs had spent Saturday morning at the office and confidentially provided the Spanish authorities with the relevant expense documents that they requested.

Then to his amazement and relief the Spanish police had told him they had it on the excellent authority of a Señor Niculoso Menendez that the firm of Stubbs and Company was completely blameless, as was a Miss Liza Summers, who had been inadvertently drawn into the plot and been instrumental in helping the capture of the thief. They had departed with the words that obviously, as the case was to be tried in Spain, it was unlikely to make the British Press, but even if it did he had nothing to fear. The names of Stubbs and Company and Miss Summers would not be made public.

Liza could not take it all in, and she sat in a daze as Mr Stubbs rattled on about how grateful he was to her. Slowly it dawned on her it was solely because of Nick's intervention she was not now languishing in a Spanish jail. He was a hero, according to Mr Stubbs. A regular, modern-day James Bond, as he so succinctly put it.

'My God, Liza, have you any idea how lucky you were? Apparently the day after you left Lanzarote the optician's receptionist was brutally beaten up by two of the gang. That's what happens when thieves begin to fall out. They look for everyone connected to the crime. They called the hotel you were staying in at Teguise, looking for you, and discovered you were in Spain with Señor Menendez—you were probably next on their list.'

'Me!' Liza's mouth fell open in shocked horror, she had seen the receptionist when she had gone to the shop, and the whole affair took on a nightmare flavour.

'Yes, my girl. Menendez had a security cordon placed

around his family home, and took you away to a safe house. He very probably saved your life, because the two villains were finally picked up four days later trying to board a flight for Malaga. A bit too close for comfort, hmm?'

Finally Mr Stubbs ended with he was bored with retirement after only two months and quite relieved to return to work, and of course Liza would resume as his secretary. But Liza wasn't listening; she was in a state of shock.

'Comfortable, darling?' Liza's mum asked as Liza fastened her seat belt. 'You look a bit pale.'

Pale wasn't the word; terrified was more like it, Liza thought drily, at what she was about to do. It was over two months since she had left Spain, and now she was going back. She tried to tell herself she was simply accepting Anna Menendez's offer to spend Easter with her mother at her home. But the reality was she was hoping to see Nick. At the very least she owed him a huge apology and quite possibly her life...

After her meeting with Mr Stubbs Liza had returned to her studio apartment in Kensington in a state of utter confusion. She accepted that, even if Nick had suspected she was involved in the diamond theft, he had gone out of his way to protect her, whisking her away from Lanzarote to Spain, and then again to the ski-cabin when he thought her life was in danger, keeping her safe while all the culprits were rounded up and, according to Mr Stubbs, persuading Carl Dalk, the owner of the diamonds, to drop any charges that could have been brought against her for acting as a courier on the island.

Rather than *the lying, lecherous apology of a man* she had called Nick. He was a hero; he had very probably saved her life or saved her from a beating. She knew everything he had done he had done for her, to protect her name and her reputation.

With the exception of the sex, she amended wryly, but Nick was a powerful, virile man; he had asked and she had agreed. And where was it written that a hero had to be celibate?

Night after sleepless night, Liza had been tormented by the memory of his lovemaking, her body hot and aching with frustration. She had let Nick think she was sophisticated about sex. She had been determined not to fall in love with him, because she was afraid of being hurt, convinced he was not the type for commitment. But now she was haunted by the thought that perhaps they could have had more than a brief affair if she had been more honest with him.

Very soon she would find out… Over the past three days Liza had spent hours preparing a speech of apology and thanks, and she was determined to deliver it in person to Nick if humanly possible; as for the rest, she could hope…

'I'm fine.' Flashing her mother a brief smile, Liza settled back in her seat, but her stomach was churning with fear and anticipation. In a few hours she would be back in Nick's family home, and hopefully see the man himself.

Seated in the small sitting room that Anna Menendez kept as her own, the greetings over, and having finished the tea that had been offered, Liza took little part in the conversation.

Her mother and Anna were so obviously delighted in each other's company she felt a bit like a third wheel. She was dying to ask if Nick was around, but did not dare.

'This must be boring for you, Liza.' Anna smiled across at her from her position next to her mother on a comfortable sofa. 'Why don't you go and freshen up, have a rest, or look around? It's a nice, sunny day.'

'Well, if you don't mind.' Liza got to her feet with alacrity; perhaps she might bump into Nick if he was here, or subtly question Manuel as to Nick's whereabouts. In her present state of nervous tension, anything was better than sitting doing nothing.

'You are in the blue room again, Liza. Manuel has already taken your luggage up. You run along; Pamela and I have a lot of gossip to catch up on.' The two older women shared a smile. 'We will see you back here about seven for drinks. Dinner is at eight. I thought a quiet meal for your first evening. There will only be the four of us, that is if Niculoso ever arrives. I have hardly seen him in the past few weeks,' Anna confided with a slight grimace.

Liza's heart missed a beat and she had to battle down a blush at the mention of his name. 'Well, he is a very busy man,' she murmured. But the uppermost thought in her mind was that she would see Nick tonight...

'So he keeps telling me, but aren't we all?' Anna turned to smile at Pam.

Knowing she would not be missed, Liza said, 'If you will excuse me,' and headed for the door.

With her blonde hair swept up into a twist on the top of her head, a few stray tendrils teased around her face and neck to soften the style, Liza donned a blue silk sheath dress. She glanced at her reflection in the mirror; spaghetti straps supported the bodice and the fabric skimmed her shapely figure to end just above her knees. Not bad, she told herself, and, slipping her feet into high-heeled sandals, she was ready.

She drew a deep, steadying breath, and left the room. Manuel directed her into the small sitting room, and she stopped. Nick was there and pouring the drinks, impeccably attired in full evening dress, his international-playboy image on display. His awesome masculine presence took her breath away, and for a moment she was unable to think of anything over the pounding of her heart.

'Ah, Liza.' Anna spoke. 'You look lovely.'

Recovering her shattered poise, Liza glanced around. Anna and her mother were seated on matching armchairs, leaving only the sofa free. 'Thank you,' she mumbled, making for the sofa and sitting down before her trembling legs betrayed her.

'Niculoso.' Anna addressed her son. 'Doesn't Liza look lovely?'

Liza lifted guarded eyes to where Nick stood by the drinks trolley. His hard dark gaze slid insolently over her, lingering for a moment on the exposed curve of her breasts before meeting hers.

'Liza.' No 'hello'—just the briefest inclination of his proud head. 'Yes, you do look beautiful.' And he stared at her so coolly she knew the compliment was for his mother's benefit, not hers. 'Would you like a drink? A white wine?'

'Yes,' Liza husked, and watched as he filled a glass with sparkling wine, looking so cold and remote that her heart sank. Then in one lithe stride he was in front of her, holding out the glass; she took it and the brush of his fingers against hers made her hand tremble.

Liza murmured, 'Thank you,' and then, gathering up what little courage she had, she added quietly, 'I would like to talk to you, Nick.' Her mother and Anna had started reminiscing yet again and it might be the only chance she had.

Lowering his long length onto the sofa beside her, his thigh inches away from her own, he relaxed back against the cushions. 'So talk.'

'I want to apologise for—' she began her speech.

'Apology accepted for whatever…' he replied curtly with a dismissive wave of one elegant hand. 'Drop the subject; it is no longer of any interest to me.'

In other words, Liza realised dismally, she was no longer of any interest to him.

Dinner was a disaster. Nick was charming to Pamela and Anna, but every time he spoke to Liza he was polite and even smiling, but the smile never reached his eyes.

Liza was relieved when the meal was over and they returned to the sitting room for a nightcap, but not for long. Within minutes her mother and Anna declared their intention of going to bed, and Anna's parting comment made Liza blush scarlet with embarrassment.

'Nick, you'd better stay the night—you have had far too much to drink and drive. Liza, I am depending on you to make sure he doesn't have any more.'

Nick laughed out loud at his mother's comment. 'I can look after myself, Mamma. Goodnight.'

'I don't think that was very funny,' Liza commented as soon as the two older women left the room. 'Your mother is worried about you.'

Nick stared down at where Liza sat, looking coolly beautiful and infinitely desirable, and he was filled with an all-consuming anger. She had turned his life inside-out, filled him with feelings he had never thought existed. He had spent the last few weeks driving himself crazy over her. He couldn't sleep or work for thinking about her. He was drinking far too much, risking far too much, and it was all her fault. Yet she sat there looking so exquisite, so calm, as if she had never had a sleepless night in her life, and so bloody sanctimonious, when he knew she could not give a fig if he broke his neck. He wanted to throttle her, but even more he wanted to lose himself in the wondrous, welcoming heat of her delectable body.

But nothing of his angry thoughts showed on his starkly handsome face as he replied, 'I thought you English were fond of irony. Does it not strike you as laughable that my mother should request you to monitor my drinking, when the last time we met you damn near killed me?'

'I said I was sorry. I want to apologise for all the awful things I said.' Liza began her speech again, horribly embarrassed and desperately ashamed of her own actions but trying to stay cool. She had to do this; she owed him big time. 'Also I want to thank you...'

Nick looked at her with hard, assessing eyes. No way was she getting away with a simple apology, not after the strain she had put him through; his pride alone would not let him accept it.

'You want to thank me,' he drawled mockingly. Their eyes met and she cringed under the savage intensity of his gaze. 'Then feel free.' His autocratic face hardened in a smile of masterly cynicism. 'But as another drink is not an option I am going to my room; you know where it is.' And with that parting shot he walked out. Nick strode along the hall, a deep frown marring his handsome face.

He had never felt so relieved when the police informed him that Liza was totally innocent. At least the scumbag Brown had had the decency to exonerate her. Not that Nick had ever doubted it really, but it meant she was free on her own merit, rather than all the strings he had had to pull to get her back to London.

He should have been happy seeing her again, but instead he had been furiously angry, and now unless she came to his room, which was highly unlikely, he had blown it again.

At first Liza was shocked into immobility, and simply sat on the sofa staring at the closed door. He had walked out on her and never even said goodnight. How could he be so rude? Then she realised how dumb she was being. Nick was a proud man. He had spent his time, and money, according to Mr Stubbs, rescuing her from the folly of her own actions, and she had fought Nick every step of the way, even to hitting him, while quite blatantly enjoying his body.

He was entitled to be offhand. What had she expected— that he would welcome her with open arms, and say all was forgiven, and declare his undying love? In her dreams maybe. But in reality it was up to her to make him listen and beg his forgiveness. She had read him so wrongly.

Her mind made up, Liza slowly got to her feet. Nick had laid down the gauntlet, and she had a quizzical notion, a bit like a knight of old, and it was up to her to take it up.

CHAPTER ELEVEN

THERE were butterflies in Liza's stomach as she reached for the door handle and, turning it, she walked in. It was a large room, and two bedside lamps illuminated a huge bed. Liza swallowed hard and stepped forward, her gaze swinging around to where a fireplace dominated one wall; the fire was lit and cast haunting shadows on the plain white walls.

Nick was standing by the window, his back towards her; he had shed his jacket and she recognised the fierce tension in his wide, taut shoulders.

'Nick.' She murmured his name and stopped a few feet away.

'So you came.' Nick turned around and rested sardonic eyes on her. 'What for, Liza?' and stopped. He had thought he wanted his pound of flesh, but as he saw her standing before him, her beautiful face pale, and her brilliant blue eyes skittering nervously around the room, glancing anywhere but at him, all he wanted to do was to reassure her. It was the same protective instinct he had in spades around her coming back with a vengeance.

'Because I want...' she almost said 'you', but stopped herself in time '...to apologise properly for all the terrible things I said to you.' The sight of him, black hair ruffled as though he had been running his hand through it, and his shirt unbuttoned to the waist, revealing the dark line of body hair vanishing beneath his low-slung trousers, captivated her senses, and she fought to remember the speech she had prepared.

She jerked her head back up to his face. 'I also want to thank you for rescuing me from a very nasty situation.'

Concentrate on his face, she told herself, but when her eyes met his she had difficulty remembering what she was going to say. 'I...I...' she stammered, stunned by the smouldering gleam in his gaze, but, lifting her chin, she continued courageously, 'I know you probably did it more for the friendship between our mothers than for me.' She had worked that out in the long hours of soul-searching before coming here. 'But I really did not know there were diamonds in the package Henry Brown asked me to deliver, and that is the honest truth. If I am guilty of anything, it is being so gullible as to do what Brown told me. A free holiday—I can't believe I fell for it.' She shook her head. 'All I can say in my defence is I had only ever worked for Mr Stubbs before, and he is a real gentleman. I naively thought Henry Brown was basically the same.'

How dumb did that make her, she thought, looking at Nick. He was her champion, her hero, and she needed to let him know his action in protecting her had not been misplaced. But, more, she needed him to believe her... She felt her hands perspiring and nervously rubbed the damp palms over her hips as she waited for his response.

Nick looked into her wary blue eyes. He was a proud man, but he wasn't a stupid one... Liza had come to him... Neither was he blind; his eyes darkened as he traced the action of her hands down her slender hips, pulling the fine fabric tight over her luscious body, and moved slowly back up to her face, missing no delectable detail on the way.

It was what he loved about her, her courage in facing him, with the same impulsive fervour she had always had, and he would not have her any other way.

'Take a seat, Liza. Relax.'

Liza breathed a little easier and sat down in the nearest armchair beside the fire and watched as Nick strolled to a cabinet against the wall and opened it.

'Would you like a drink? A nightcap?' he offered.

'Is that wise?' Liza felt bound to say.

'I have rarely been wise around you,' Nick said quietly,

and, filling two glasses with amber liquid, he walked over to her and handed her one, before lowering his long length into the chair opposite and lifting the crystal glass to his mouth.

Liza eyed him warily, and tentatively took a sip of her drink before placing it on the table. She leaned forward. 'I want to explain,' she said earnestly, trying once again for her speech. 'I really had no idea Henry Brown was a thief, Nick, and when you brought me here…I actually thought it was for your mother's benefit. But I want you to know, I'm not a complete idiot. I did suspect there was something wrong. And all I can say is after I got back to London and Mr Stubbs told me the full story I was mortified.' She took another drink of the brandy, to give her the courage to go on, and looked back at Nick.

'I now know not only did you save me from a possible prison sentence, you also probably saved my life, when you had no real reason to trust me. So I want to thank you from…' the bottom of my heart, she had been going to say but never got the chance.

'Stop right there, Liza,' Nick cut in, his dark eyes capturing hers. 'First I don't think I ever really believed you were a thief, Liza. When your name appeared on a report from a security agency of mine that was investigating the diamond theft, my immediate reaction was to fly to Lanzarote and question you for myself.' Nick told her honestly, 'I admit, I did it in a slightly devious way, but that was because I had to protect the interests of Carl Dalk, and, though you didn't know it, you had information that was vital to solving the case.'

'You're right. I never knew.'

'I know.' Nick rose to his feet and moved to stand in front of her, looking down into her beautiful, slightly pink face. He should not have given her the brandy on top of the wine she had already drunk, and, reaching for her hand, he pulled her to her feet.

'I brought you back to Spain with me to keep you out

of harm's way, and also because I wanted you. I also know, when I was driving you up to the cabin, I have never been more terrified in my life for your safety, nor more certain you were absolutely innocent.' Liza was still reeling from his casual admission *I wanted you* when he continued. 'We both made mistakes, so what say we call a truce, forget about the criminal case altogether and see where we go from here?'

'A truce.' Liza swallowed hard; it couldn't be that easy. 'Yes. OK.'

'Sealed with a kiss,' Nick prompted. His arm went round her back and arched her body to meet his as his lips met hers in a burning open-mouthed kiss. Nick made a husky sound, almost a groan, and Liza quivered helplessly under the insistent pressure of his savagely hungry mouth. She closed her eyes, and reached for him, her hands curving around his broad shoulders. She could not deny the need, the desire scorching through her, didn't want to, as she silently admitted what she had been trying to deny for months—she loved him…

'*Dios,* Liza,' Nick muttered, his palm cupping her breast, a thumb stroking her nipple through the fine fabric of her dress, and a low moan of pleasure escaped her. 'Have you any idea what you do to me?' he queried softly, his hand sliding down her thigh and urging her against his strong, hard body, making her achingly aware of just how much he wanted her.

Black eyes gleaming with sensual amusement held hers. 'Do you think you are brave enough to get over *two* mothers in the house, or are you going to make me wait until we can get away for a night or two?' Nick drawled hardly.

As the import of his words sank in Liza felt the shock drain the heat from her body. She stiffened and pulled back. 'Wait.' She placed her hand against his chest, pushing him away.

Nick was doing it again—*apology accepted, OK, let's go to bed.* No mention of a future, no mention of love. Twice he had seduced her into his bed and she was not falling for it a third time. She was worth more than that.

She had spent weeks getting up the nerve to face him, and tonight over dinner he had virtually ignored her. But still she had got up the courage to face him in his room, at his request, because she thought she had hurt his pride and owed him a proper apology. He might have saved her life, but that did not mean he could use her.

'You aren't really going to make me wait.' Nick reached for her, and she slapped his hand away.

'Liza.' Nick's dark eyes clashed with hers. 'What's going on here?'

'Nothing. I came to apologise and I have.' She saw the incredulous look on his face, the flash of fury in his eyes, but she refused to be intimidated. 'Thanks for your offer, but no.'

'But you want me; your body doesn't lie and you know how good we are together,' Nick growled, flicking a glance at the taut outline of her nipples against the fabric of her dress. He wasn't mistaken—a moment ago she had melted in his arms, so what had gone wrong?

'Maybe, but I find I want more from a relationship than just hot sex, and you're not the type,' Liza said flatly, 'but I'm sure we can remain friends for the sake of our mothers.' She looked up and for a second she thought she saw a look of pain in his night-black eyes.

'So be it.' And with a shrug of his broad shoulders Nick walked to the door and held it open. 'Run along, *friend*,' he drawled sarcastically.

She had done the right thing, Liza told herself an hour later, tossing restlessly in her own bed. The only trouble was she could remember all too vividly Nick making love to her in the same bed, and she burned with frustrated desire until finally she fell into a troubled sleep.

In the room next door Nick downed another brandy, and, slamming the glass down on the table, he muttered, 'To hell with it.' Liza was never going to be his again; she had made that very plain—*he was not her type*. No woman had ever told him that before. It was ironic it had to come from the one woman he truly wanted.

Never mind, he would do what he had planned to do before he knew she was coming. He was flying to Switzerland tomorrow, to take part in the Verbier run.

Anna and her mother were halfway though their breakfast by the time Liza made it to the dining room.

'You look like hell,' her mother said.

'Thanks, Mum. Good morning, Anna,' she greeted the pair of them and sat down at the table, but she wasn't hungry.

'There is nothing good about it,' Anna said bluntly. 'I thought when Nick agreed to come to dinner last night with you and Pam, he might have given up on the Verbier run tomorrow, though I knew he had entered it.'

Liza's face paled; the Verbier run—she had heard of it and seen it on television. It was a death-defying snow-boarder's race in the Alps at the end of the extreme-sport season. 'Oh, no.'

'Exactly, Liza.' Anna's brown eyes met Liza's appalled blue. 'He left here this morning hell-bent on taking part; he is flying to Switzerland this afternoon. I told him not to be so crazy.' She shrugged. 'But he takes no notice of me. I don't know what happened between you two last night, but you must have said something to upset him.'

'Me, upset him?' Liza exclaimed.

Her own mother chipped in, 'Anna and I went to bed at a ridiculously early hour so the pair of you could be alone, so what went wrong?'

Liza could not believe what she was hearing. 'You... She...' She looked from one to the other, and they both stared back at her with bland faces. 'You tried to set me up? To set *us* up?'

'Certainly. I know what has been going on between you, Nick and Carl Dalk,' Anna said firmly, and Liza's face turned scarlet. For a moment she thought his mother knew they were lovers, until she added, 'My son is not the only one with friends in high places.'

'You know about the diamond theft?' Liza asked hesitantly, hoping that was all they knew.

'Yes, and don't worry, your mother knows as well,' Anna confirmed. 'And from what I can gather Nick rescued you from a very awkward situation. All your mother and I were doing last night was giving you a chance to thank Nick in person, because according to my chauffeur, Lancio, you and Nick did not part on the best of terms.'

'You should have told me Liza,' her mother cut in. 'And I do hope you have thanked Nick properly.'

'Yes, I did, Mother,' Liza murmured, and she wondered what her mother would say if she told her the truth. Nick did not want to be thanked properly, but very improperly, if the scene in his bedroom last night was anything to go by.

'Leave the poor girl alone, Pam. Can't you see she is embarrassed?' Anne prompted and reaching across the table took Liza's hand in hers.

'I know my own son, he is a hard man, he allows very few people to get close to him. But has a soft spot for you, Liza, or why else would he have helped you out of that mess in January? So I was wondering if you would try and talk Nick out of going to Verbier? Myself, Manuel, everyone has tried, and the stubborn fool takes no notice. I have no desire to see my only child, dead or paralysed in the name of sport. You are my last hope, Liza, and you will be doing me a huge favour if you can stop him.'

Her imagination running riot, a vision of Nick's magnificent body crushed and broken at the foot of a snow-covered cliff filled Liza's mind. And she knew she couldn't bear it if anything happened to him. Whether she was with him or not, it didn't make any difference. She should have realised that when she watched Nick para-skiing, and decided not to let herself love him. Love was not something you could take or leave. It was inside you, filling every atom of your being, and if you were really lucky your love was returned.

Nick had not offered her everlasting love the night before, but he had offered her a relationship of sorts and she had turned him down, too frightened of getting hurt. Yet she was a hundred times more terrified of Nick getting hurt, and the realisation made everything clear. She loved him totally unselfishly. Whether he was with her for a day or a lifetime, she was going to take a chance.

'I'll try,' Liza said; she had been a coward for far too long, hiding her emotions. If she wanted Nick's love she had to take a chance and ask for it. 'Just tell me how to find him.'

'We can do better than that,' her mother said, giving her a gentle smile. 'Manuel is waiting with the car to take you to the airport. Nick's plane is scheduled to leave at one.'

It was the longest ride of her life; she watched the clock on the dashboard ticking away the seconds and minutes, willing Manuel to drive faster.

Finally at twenty to one she leapt out of the car at the airport.

She dashed in to the building and scanned the crowd and her heart fell to her feet. There was no way she was going to find Nick's plane in time. She rushed to the information desk and was directed to the VIP lounge, only to find when she got there, breathless and panting, that she was refused entry. Swinging frantically around, panic setting in as to what to do next, Liza slammed into a hard body.

'Sorry.' She tried to step back and found her lace top was caught in a jacket button; she grasped it with her finger and looked up. 'Nick!'

'You appear to be attached to me,' he mocked, his dark eyes roaming leisurely over her, lingering on the wide blue eyes, and lower to her lush, trembling mouth.

He lifted a hand to cover hers, still grasping the button

of his jacket. 'Care to tell me what you are doing here, Liza?'

For a long moment she just looked at him as she struggled to catch her breath, her heart aching. 'I came to find you,' she finally said.

His dark, brooding glance narrowed fractionally on her face. 'Why?'

'Because I love you, and I don't want you to do the Ver…Ver…Verbier run,' she stammered on a long, shuddering sigh, but she had said it. His dark eyes look steadily down at her and she began to wonder if he had heard her at all.

Then he moved, his arms locking around her. 'What do you want me to do instead, Liza?' he demanded curtly. 'Something like this?'

His black head bent towards her and his mouth covered hers, and her lips parted to welcome the probing warmth of his tongue. A fierce, primitive pleasure swept through her as she wrapped her arms around his neck and pressed into his hard body.

'I seem to remember you said last night I was not your type, Liza,' Nick prompted, easing her away from him. 'What made you change your mind?'

He had not jumped at her declaration of love. In fact she was shocked by the fierce tension evident in every line of his body and she had to think for a second what he was talking about. 'No, no I said *you* were not *the* type. I meant for commitment,' she scrambled to explain. 'But it's not important to me any more. I want you—a day, a week, anything I can get.'

The transformation from cold arrogance to glittering triumph was spectacular. 'You'd better mean what you say, Liza,' Nick declared adamantly, black eyes blazing. 'Because I am never letting you go again,' and he captured her mouth with his own in a wildly possessive kiss.

When Nick finally let her breathe again, she heard the sound of clapping. Her wide blue eyes, lit with love, looked into his. 'I think we have gathered an audience.' And they both burst out laughing.

'Let's get out of here,' Nick murmured and turned, but one side of his jacket was still caught on Liza's blouse. He wrapped an arm around her waist and, hugging her to his side, they left the airport. Manuel grinned when he saw them, and with a flourish opened the rear door of the car.

Liza suddenly stopped dead on the pavement. 'Wait, Nick.'

'Changed your mind again?' Nick closed his eyes for a moment. 'I don't believe it.'

'No.' Liza smiled and slid into the back seat. 'I forgot—you must call your mother; she will be worried sick.'

He called on his mobile from the car, and thirty minutes later Liza was standing in the hall of his Malaga home.

'It's beautiful, Nick.' High ceilings, the floor a marble mosaic, and the central staircase white marble. She glanced at him; he had removed his jacket when they got in the car, and his white tailored shirt fitted snugly across his broad shoulders, contrasting with his tanned sculptured features.

Nick stepped in front of her. 'My beautiful Liza.' And he lifted a hand to brush gentle fingers across her cheek. 'Are you going to make me wait again?'

'Well, maybe,' she said, a bubble of laughter emerging from her throat at the brief appalled expression on his handsome face. 'Until you find a bed.'

'Witch.' His eyes gleamed with humour and a deep sensual passion as he lifted her in his arms and carried her up the grand staircase.

She put one arm around his neck and with her other hand set her fingers to work on the buttons of his shirt. By the time he shouldered the bedroom door open, and finally placed her back on her feet by the side of a large bed, his shirt was hanging off him.

He stripped off the rest of his clothes, and hers, and they fell onto the bed in a tangle of arms and legs. Nick's mouth found hers and the kiss was like no other, deep and tender and then very quickly flaming out of control.

'I can't wait Liza…it has been too long,' Nick growled, raising his head, his dark eyes burning into hers as he nudged apart her legs and moved between her thighs.

Liza slid her arms around his neck and clenched her hands in his black hair. 'Then what's stopping you?' she said urgently. Naked flesh on flesh, she burned with a need, an ache that was almost pain.

The hunger, the need seemed to explode as Nick's mouth met hers, and they were engulfed in a tidal wave of wild primitive passion. Nick's hands and mouth were all over her body, caressing her heated flesh in a frenzy of possessive need, as if he would devour her whole. Liza heard her own wild moans even as she gloried in the husky growls she drew from him with her own frantic caresses of his magnificent body.

'Liza.' Nick rasped her name and her ecstatic cry mingled with his as she met and matched the driving rhythm of his incredible body, totally possessed. They climaxed as one in seismic convulsions savage in intensity that left them spent and shuddering uncontrollably in each other's arms.

For a long moment the only sound was the tortured breathing of two sated bodies. Eventually Nick rolled onto his back and, curving an arm around Liza's shoulders, pulled her close and leaned over her. 'I needed that; I needed you.' His smile was slightly uncertain. 'Are you all right?'

Liza smiled radiantly back. 'Never better.' She saw the familiar confidence return to his slumberous black eyes.

'I was amazed when I saw you at the airport,' Nick offered softly. 'But I'm glad you came.' He brushed his hand through the strands of blonde hair falling over her face, stroking them out against the pillow. 'I dreamt of your hair on my pillow again,' he murmured throatily. 'You drive me crazy, Liza. I just have to see you to want you. You're so exquisite.' He glanced down at the languorous curve of her naked body, then back again, his dark eyes serious as they caught and held hers.

'I love you. I love everything about you—from your incredible hair to your sexy body.' Rubbing his chin, he added, 'Even your left hook I decided was better than no contact at all in the two long months we've been apart. How desperate is that?' he joked.

Liza tensed in shock; was she dreaming, or had he finally said he loved her?

Nick felt her tense. 'Are you OK?' he asked, his dark eyes, full of concern, searching her beautiful face. 'I didn't hurt you?'

Lifting her hand, she cupped the strong line of his jaw. 'No, you didn't hurt me.' There had been too many half-truths between them, but now there was no need. 'I loved every second,' she said softly, her blue eyes wide as she met his concerned gaze and saw the flare of pleasure in his eyes.

'And I am so sorry for hitting you that day. I would have died if anything happened to you. You were always my hero as a child,' she told him honestly, wrapped safely in his strong arms. 'Then, after the episode in the stables, I tried to hate you. But as soon as I met you again in Lanzarote and you kissed me I knew I was lost.'

'You and I both.' Nick groaned. 'I love you to the point of desperation.' And he sank back on the bed, hauling her over him and kissing her so urgently she had to pull back eventually.

'Nick, I need to breathe.' Draped over his broad chest, she looked down into his darkly attractive face, and she saw the passion mixed with tenderness and love in his night-black eyes. 'You really love me?' she prompted, and she could feel his heart bounding in his broad chest, her own almost bursting with love.

A large hand slid around the nape of her neck and tangled in the long length of her hair. 'Never doubt it, Liza. I can't begin to tell you how much.'

'Enough to forget about the Verbier run?' she teased but with a hint of anxiety.

'Enough to forget about everything except you,' he ascertained. But he could still sense her slight insecurity and he determined to leave her in no doubt at all of his feelings. 'I loved you as a child of eight, but I fell in love with you as a man when you were sixteen.'

'What?' Liza exclaimed. 'I don't believe you.'

Nick chuckled. His hand was around her narrow waist, and she folded her arms over his broad chest and rested her chin on them, fascinated and intrigued as he continued.

'I noticed you were turning into a women the summer you were fourteen, but you were still young Liza, my pal. The next summer was different. When we were out riding and you fell from your horse.'

'I remember that,' Liza inserted. 'You were so kind.'

'Kind was not how I felt,' Nick said drily. 'I thought you were dead, and it hit me like a ton of bricks. I couldn't imagine a world without you in it.' His hand tightened on her waist. 'I should have known then that I was falling in love with you. But I arrogantly dismissed the feelings you aroused in me, as a simple reaction to the shock at the thought of the loss of a friend's life, nothing more.'

'And the next summer you were engaged to Sophia.' Liza frowned.

'Yes,' Nick sighed. 'I told you about that, but with hindsight, it was not just for my father's benefit I got engaged to Sophia. I think subconsciously I knew that the way I felt about you when you had your accident was dangerous. You were far too young for me, and the engagement was not just to protect my father, but myself.'

'But you slept with her,' Liza could not help adding.

'No, I didn't. Sophia is more interested in women.' He gave her a slanted smile. 'I am a lot older than you, so there have been other women in my life, but you are the only one I have ever loved or ever will.'

Somehow what he had told her about Sophia didn't surprise her; it made sense of the convenient engagement. 'But that day in the stable, when you saw me...' She trailed off. Why had he been so angry?

As if reading her mind, Nick said, 'I knew my engagement to Sophia was a convenience, nothing more. But seeing you kissing that spotty young boy, I was eaten up with jealousy because it should have been me. I suddenly realised I had always thought in the back of my mind that one day you and I would get together and I was furious. But I could do nothing about it, which is why I lashed out at you.' He kissed her hard and fast, as though to expunge the memory.

'But if what you say is true why did you never look me up later?' she asked when she could get her breath back.

Nick made a wry face, and, rolling her over onto her back, he eased a long leg over her slender limbs, so she was pinned beneath him. He was taking no more chances. 'Because, sweet Liza,' he said, smiling crookedly, 'I only recognised the truth after I met you again. I could not help trying to protect you, but even after we became lovers I told myself it was just another affair. It was at the cabin that I finally admitted to myself I loved you.'

'Why, you... Talk about spinning a line.' She wriggled against him, but he laughingly held her firm, and his hairy chest rubbing against her breast sent a tingling awareness from her head to her toes.

'Do you want me to go on?' Nick drawled huskily. 'Or shall I prove I love you another way?' And she felt his great body stirring against her belly.

'Keep talking,' she said, her heart beating fast as she watched him through the thick curl of her lashes, a half-smile curving her lips.

'Spoilsport,' he chuckled. 'Well, you know I came to Lanzarote looking for you. And as soon as I saw you at that café I wanted you. I still needed the information, but I convinced Carl to let me take care of you. The very first night at my villa I decided I didn't care what you had or had not done, I was not having you involved, and I got you to come to Spain.'

'And seduced me on the plane!' Liza gave him a teasing look. 'But I admit I wanted to be seduced. I had had a crush on you since I was fourteen, and when you got engaged I was devastated—more so when you caught me in the stable and called me a slut. I decided I hated you, but then at your villa I agreed to go to see your mother in Spain, and at the same time decided you could be my holiday romance if nothing else.'

'I surprised myself on the plane,' Nick confessed drily. 'I am not the womaniser the Press makes me out to be. I am usually the most restrained of men, and that was the first and only time I have made love on the jet. But as for the holiday romance...' His voice deepened and his arms tightened around her. 'I like the idea, as long as it is a holiday romance that lasts a lifetime, with you as my wife. Do you agree?'

Liza's blue eyes widened in amazement on his. Nick was stripped of the cold, arrogant persona he usually showed the world, and she saw the uncertainty in the darkening depths of his eyes, the vulnerability, and her heart overflowed with love for him. 'Yes, I agree—though it wasn't the most romantic proposal in the world,' she teased.

Nick grinned, and raised a finger and brushed her cheek. 'But it worked, and I won't let you out of my sight until you have my ring on your finger.' He held her closer and his mouth moved on hers in a kiss of tender worshipful possession. 'We will marry as soon as possible.'

'Yes,' Liza breathed, and looked into his deep dark eyes. She saw they had a fire burning in them, a dark all-consuming fire in which she saw herself reflected. 'My hero...' she sighed, and reached for him.

Four hours later Liza turned as Nick strolled back into the bedroom, looking stunning in dark trousers, a blue shirt, and a cashmere sweater draped loosely over his broad shoulders. 'I thought you said five minutes.' He grinned, and Liza's heart-rate speeded up.

'Do I look all right?' she asked, shoving back the over-long shirtsleeves. Her own top was torn, and she was wearing one of Nick's shirts over her hipster jeans.

'I am not going to answer that on the grounds we will never get out of here if I start thinking exactly how delectable you are. Come on.' And, catching her hand, he led her downstairs and out of the house.

Twenty minutes later Nick ushered Liza into a very exclusive jewellers. The proprietor knew Nick, and in moments they were seated in deep-cushioned velvet chairs beside a glass-topped table, and an assistant was asking them what they would like to drink. Coffee, Champagne...

Nick ordered both.

'Do we have to do this now?' Liza demurred, intimidated by the hushed opulence of the place.

'It's up to you,' Nick said reasonably, his fingers caressing her palm. 'If you want to appear ringless at dinner tonight in front of the two mothers I don't mind.' He smiled into Liza's eyes while tightening his hold on her hand. 'After you insisted at the airport I phoned Mamma and I told her you had persuaded me to give up the Verbier run, and all other extreme sports, she was delighted,' he said casually. 'In fact, she was almost speechless when I told her I was thinking of indulging in more indoor sports, and I was taking you home with me for a siesta as befitted a man of my age,' he ended with devilish mockery.

'You didn't!' Liza exclaimed in horror. Looking into his dark eyes, she saw the wicked golden sparks and groaned. 'Oh, no, you did.' She turned scarlet.

Nick was still grinning at the expression on Liza's face when the proprietor reappeared with a tray of exquisite diamond rings. He felt her hand jerk in his, and the grin swiftly turned into a grimace. Diamonds were not a good idea, under the circumstances. The last thing Liza needed was a constant reminder of the diamond heist. How insensitive was that?

'I'm sorry, Liza.' He turned her face towards him with a hand at her chin. 'I never thought. Why don't you choose something else?'

For once the tables were turned and her indomitable lover was looking less than his usual confident self. Lifting her free hand, she patted his cheek, taking full advantage of his obvious discomfort. 'Oh, I don't know,' Liza said slowly, her eyes gleaming with repressed amusement. 'I have become rather fond of diamonds—they will always remind me of you, Nick, darling.'

He didn't need Liza remembering every day of their married life that he had thought, just for a second, that she was a thief! 'No, please—what about sapphires, rubies, or emeralds—take your pick,' Nick said adamantly.

'Well, I don't know,' she teased, her blue eyes dancing. But, suddenly conscious of the very real anxiety in his haunted expression, she decided to put him out of his misery.

Liza tightened her fingers around his hand and leant towards him. 'If it wasn't for diamonds we would never have met again, and you did rescue me from a band of thieves,' she said quietly. 'My boss Mr Stubbs was right about you. You are a regular James Bond.' And, closing the remaining space between them, she murmured, 'I seem to remember diamonds are forever.' And she kissed him. 'And I am yours forever.'

A shout of laughter and then a dazzling smile flashed across Nick's darkly handsome features. Then he lifted her hand and pressed a kiss to her palm almost reverently. 'As I am yours—always.'

The world's bestselling romance series.

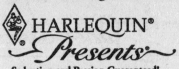

HARLEQUIN®
Presents~

Seduction and Passion Guaranteed!

Your dream ticket to the vacation of a lifetime!

Why not relax and allow Harlequin Presents® to whisk you away
to stunning international locations with our new miniseries...

FOREIGN AFFAIRS

Where irresistible men and sophisticated women surrender to seduction under the golden sun.

Don't miss this opportunity to experience glamorous lifestyles and exotic settings in:

**Robyn Donald's
THE TEMPTRESS OF TARIKA BAY**
on sale July, #2336

THE FRENCH COUNT'S MISTRESS
by Susan Stephens
on sale August, #2342

THE SPANIARD'S WOMAN
by Diana Hamilton
on sale September, #2346

THE ITALIAN MARRIAGE
by Kathryn Ross
on sale October, #2353

FOREIGN AFFAIRS... A world full of passion!

**Pick up a Harlequin Presents® novel and you will enter a world
of spine-tingling passion and provocative, tantalizing romance!**

Available wherever Harlequin books are sold.

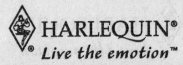

HARLEQUIN®
Live the emotion™

Visit us at www.eHarlequin.com

HPFAMA

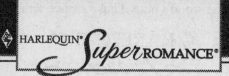

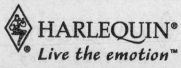

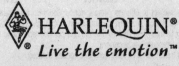

If you enjoyed what you just read,
then we've got an offer you can't resist!

Take 2 bestselling love stories FREE!

Plus get a FREE surprise gift!

Is your man too good to be true?

Hot, gorgeous AND romantic?
If so, he could be a Harlequin® Blaze™ series cover model!

Our grand-prize winners will receive a trip for two to New York City to
shoot the cover of a Blaze novel, and will stay at the luxurious Plaza Hotel.
Plus, they'll receive $500 U.S. spending money!
The runner-up winners will receive $200 U.S.
to spend on a romantic dinner for two.

It's easy to enter!

In 100 words or less, tell us what makes your boyfriend or spouse a true romantic
and the perfect candidate for the cover of a Blaze novel, and include in your submission
two photos of this potential cover model.

All entries must include the written submission of the contest entrant, two photographs of the model
candidate and the Official Entry Form and Publicity Release forms completed in full and signed by
both the model candidate and the contest entrant. Harlequin, along with the experts at
Elite Model Management, will select a winner.

For photo and complete Contest details, please refer to the Official Rules on the next page. All entries
will become the property of Harlequin Enterprises Ltd. and are not returnable.

**Please visit www.blazecovermodel.com to download a copy of the Official Entry Form and
Publicity Release Form or send a request to one of the addresses below.**

Please mail your entry to: **Harlequin Blaze Cover Model Search**

In U.S.A.	In Canada
P.O. Box 9069	P.O. Box 637
Buffalo, NY	Fort Erie, ON
14269-9069	L2A 5X3

No purchase necessary. Contest open to Canadian and U.S. residents who are 18 and over.
Void where prohibited. Contest closes September 30, 2003.

HBCVRMODEL1

HARLEQUIN BLAZE COVER MODEL SEARCH CONTEST 3569 OFFICIAL RULES
NO PURCHASE NECESSARY TO ENTER

1. To enter, submit two (2) 4" x 6" photographs of a boyfriend or spouse (who must be 18 years of age or older) taken no later than three (3) months from the time of entry: a close-up, waist up, shirtless photograph; and a fully clothed, full-length photograph, then, tell us, in 100 words or fewer, why he should be a Harlequin Blaze cover model and how he is romantic. Your complete "entry" must include: (i) your essay, (ii) the Official Entry Form and Publicity Release Form printed below completed and signed by you (as "Entrant"), (iii) the photographs (with your hand-written name, address and phone number, and your model's name, address and phone number on the back of each photograph), and (iv) the Publicity Release Form and Photograph Representation Form printed below completed and signed by your model (as "Model"), and should be sent via first-class mail to either: Harlequin Blaze Cover Model Search Contest 3569, P.O. Box 9069, Buffalo, NY, 14269-9069, or Harlequin Blaze Cover Model Search Contest 3569, P.O. Box 637, Fort Erie, Ontario L2A 5X3. All submissions must be in English and be received no later than September 30, 2003. Limit: one entry per person, household or organization. **Purchase or acceptance of a product offer does not improve your chances of winning.** All entry requirements must be strictly adhered to for eligibility and to ensure fairness among entries.

2. Ten (10) Finalist submissions (photographs and essays) will be selected by a panel of judges consisting of members of the Harlequin editorial, marketing and public relations staff, as well as a representative from Elite Model Management (Toronto) Inc., based on the following criteria:

Aptness/Appropriateness of submitted photographs for a Harlequin Blaze cover—70%
Originality of Essay—20%
Sincerity of Essay—10%

In the event of a tie, duplicate finalists will be selected. The photographs submitted by finalists will be posted on the Harlequin website no later than November 15, 2003 (at www.blazecovermodel.com), and viewers may vote, in rank order, on their favorite(s) to assist in the panel of judges' final determination of the Grand Prize and Runner-up winning entries based on the above judging criteria. All decisions of the judges are final.

3. All entries become the property of Harlequin Enterprises Ltd. and none will be returned. Any entry may be used for future promotional purposes. Elite Model Management (Toronto) Inc. and/or its partners, subsidiaries and affiliates operating as "Elite Model Management" will have access to all entries including all personal information, and may contact any Entrant and/or Model in its sole discretion for their own business purposes. Harlequin and Elite Model Management (Toronto) Inc. are separate entities with no legal association or partnership whatsoever having no power to bind or obligate the other or create any expressed or implied obligation or responsibility on behalf of the other, such that Harlequin shall not be responsible in any way for any acts or omissions of Elite Model Management (Toronto) Inc. or its partners, subsidiaries and affiliates in connection with the Contest or otherwise and Elite Model Management shall not be responsible in any way for any acts or omissions of Harlequin or its partners, subsidiaries and affiliates in connection with the contest or otherwise.

4. All Entrants and Models must be residents of the U.S. or Canada, be 18 years of age or older, and have no prior criminal convictions. The contest is not open to any Model that is a professional model and/or actor in any capacity at the time of the entry. Contest void wherever prohibited by law; all applicable laws and regulations apply. Any litigation within the Province of Quebec regarding the conduct or organization of a publicity contest may be submitted to the Régie des alcools, des courses et des jeux for a ruling, and any litigation regarding the awarding of a prize may be submitted to the Régie only for the purpose of helping the parties reach a settlement. Employees and immediate family members of Harlequin Enterprises Ltd., D.L. Blair, Inc., Elite Model Management (Toronto) Inc. and their parents, affiliates, subsidiaries and all other agencies, entities and persons connected with the use, marketing or conduct of this Contest are not eligible to enter. Acceptance of any prize offered constitutes permission to use Entrants' and Models' names, essay submissions, photographs or other likenesses for the purposes of advertising, trade, publication and promotion on behalf of Harlequin Enterprises Ltd., its parent, affiliates, subsidiaries, assigns and other authorized entities involved in the judging and promotion of the contest without further compensation to any Entrant or Model, unless prohibited by law.

5. Finalists will be determined no later than October 30, 2003. Prize Winners will be determined no later than January 31, 2004. Grand Prize Winners (consisting of winning Entrant and Model) will be required to sign and return Affidavit of Eligibility/Release of Liability and Model Release forms within thirty (30) days of notification. Non-compliance with this requirement and within the specified time period will result in disqualification and an alternate will be selected. Any prize notification returned as undeliverable will result in the awarding of the prize to an alternate set of winners. All travelers (or parent/legal guardian of a minor) must execute the Affidavit of Eligibility/Release of Liability prior to ticketing and must possess required travel documents (e.g. valid photo ID) where applicable. Travel dates specified by Sponsor but no later than May 30, 2004.

6. Prizes: One (1) Grand Prize—the opportunity for the Model to appear on the cover of a paperback book from the Harlequin Blaze series, and a 3 day/2 night trip for two (Entrant and Model) to New York, NY for the photo shoot of Model which includes round-trip coach air transportation from the commercial airport nearest the winning Entrant's home to New York, NY, (or, in lieu of air transportation, $100 cash payable to Entrant and Model, if the winning Entrant's home is within 250 miles of New York, NY), hotel accommodations (double occupancy) at the Plaza Hotel and $500 cash spending money payable to Entrant and Model, (approximate prize value: $8,000), and one (1) Runner-up Prize of $200 cash payable to Entrant and Model for a romantic dinner for two (approximate prize value: $200). Prizes are valued in U.S. currency. Prizes consist of only those items listed as part of the prize. No substitution of prize(s) permitted by winners. All prizes are awarded jointly to the Entrant and Model of the winning entries, and are not severable - prizes and obligations may not be assigned or transferred. Any change to the Entrant and/or Model of the winning entries will result in disqualification and an alternate will be selected. Taxes on prize are the sole responsibility of winners. Any and all expenses and/or items not specifically described as part of the prize are the sole responsibility of winners. Harlequin Enterprises Ltd. and D.L. Blair, Inc., their parents, affiliates, and subsidiaries are not responsible for errors in printing of Contest entries and/or game pieces. No responsibility is assumed for lost, stolen, late, illegible, incomplete, inaccurate, non-delivered, postage due or misdirected mail or entries. In the event of printing or other errors which may result in unintended prize values or duplication of prizes, all affected game pieces or entries shall be null and void.

7. Winners will be notified by mail. For winners' list (available after March 31, 2004), send a self-addressed, stamped envelope to: Harlequin Blaze Cover Model Search Contest 3569 Winners, P.O. Box 4200, Blair, NE 68009-4200, or refer to the Harlequin website (at www.blazecovermodel.com).

Contest sponsored by Harlequin Enterprises Ltd., P.O. Box 9042, Buffalo, NY 14269-9042.

HBCVRMODEL2

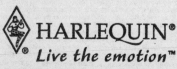